PENGUIN BOOKS

A SITUATION IN NEW DELHI

Nayantara Sahgal is a novelist and political journalist who has published two volumes of autobiography and seven novels, of which, *Rich Like Us,* won the Sinclair Prize for Fiction in 1985. She lives in Dehra Dun, India, and her chief involvement outside writing is with the civil liberties movement launched during the Emergency.

D0731423

Nayantara Sahgal

A Situation in New Delhi

PENGUIN BOOKS

Penguin Books (India) Ltd, 72-B Himalaya House,
23 Kasturba Gandhi Marg, New Delhi-110 001. India
Penguin Books Ltd, Harmondsworth, Middlesex, England
Viking Penguin Inc. 40 West 23rd Street,
New York, New York 10010, U.S.A.
Penguin Books Australia Ltd. Ringwood, Victoria, Australia
Penguin Books Canada Ltd, 2801 John Street,
Markham, Ontario, Canada L3R 1B4
Penguin Books (N.Z.) Ltd, 182-190 Wairau Road,
Auckland 10, New Zealand

First published by London Magazine Editions 1977
Published in Penguin Books 1988
Reprinted 1988
Copyright © Nayantara Sahgal 1977, 1988

Made and Printed in India by Ananda Offset Private Ltd, Calcutta.

To Ronald Sampson with affection and admiration

I

Shivraj was dead. Michael Calvert saw the news immediately he unfolded the newspaper – not in a banner headline on top – that was reserved for British calamities – but thick print halfway down the page under an astonishingly alive picture. Michael was electrified, his attention riveted to the picture and the columns under it, their impact shuddering through him. The print came up in sharp jagged points and dissolved and the paper slipped from his grasp to the floor. He sat down heavily at the table in the dining alcove, dropped his head to his arms and wept violently. Glassy-eyed and hot in the face he raised his head at last and looked down onto the green English field just below his window, where children were playing football. Enclosed in iron latticework painted a matching green, the field had a passage alongside, a shortcut to the new supermarket in Bloomsbury. People were walking through it this frosty, early spring morning, young women in bright coats briskly pushing strollers carrying rosy bundled babies; old ladies, safe here from traffic, making slower intrepid progress, their string and plastic bags on their wrists. Oblivious to it all, a sturdy young couple in fleece-lined duffle jackets stood motionless lip to lip at the entrance to the passage, Anaesthetized by his weeping, and a little resentful about life continuing, Michael picked up the newspaper, spread it on the table, and opened it to the editorial page, reading first the gravely fulsome editorial that recognized too late one of God's remarkable creations. Michael turned the pages to the generously worded obituary, and columns of comment from here and Europe and across the Atlantic, by everyone of consequence. Western opinion, paraded in all its adjectival array, now that Shivraj was dead. They hadn't paid much attention to him while he lived. The experts who knew all about democracy and had, by the way they talked, invented it out of one of their cursed computer machines, had led the chorus prophesying chaos instead of supporting his Herculean labours. Nor had the other side given Shivraj his due. The Communist monolith, before it broke in two, had pelted him with its dreary bagful of clichés. Michael's bitterness overwhelmed him, consoling in its exaggeration. An Asian who believed there was a middle road had evidently been an insult to both sides.

Michael had instinctively thought of Shivraj as an Asian, not an Indian. For that, far ahead of an Asian actuality, was what he had been: a symbol of the fight against colonial rule, a hero who had re-surrected a legend so much of Asia shared and given it modern meaning – renouncing gilded ease to sleep on prison planks. A leader – *the* leader – at least in inspiration, of so many beyond his own borders. And for Indians, a man who took the people with him on uncharted journeys, on the frail, unbreakable, so very unpolitical bond of trust. A politician who till the day he died had never learned to make a political speech, or to trim his sails by the exigen-cies of politics. No spell weaver himself, he had never trusted the breed. The spells he had woven had been unintended. Like it or not, Michael told the printed pages spread before him, there isn't going to be another like him in a hundred years.

The telephone rang. He got up with difficulty, moving slowly to answer it, as if years had added themselves to his frame. He spoke numbly into the receiver.

'Is that you, Michael? You sound as though you had a cold. Sad news today about Shivraj,' a pause and then, 'I have one or two sug-gestions to make about your last two chapters.'

Michael was unable to make the mental shift. 'Shivraj is dead,' he said.

'Yes, it's a shock and an unbelievable loss. He was too young to die. No age at all.'

'He is dead,' Michael repeated and hung up.

A minute later he was dialling his publisher's number.

'What happened?' asked John Drexel in surprise, 'I thought you'd hung up.'

Yes, I did hang up, thought Michael in a spasm of anger. Of course I hung up. This is my day of fierce mourning and it should bloody well be yours. We shall never see his like again.

'I'm sorry,' he spoke bleakly into the mouthpiece, wholly contrite

6

because John Drexel was an old and valued friend, 'What were you saying?'

'I was about to suggest lunch today. The manuscript is in perfect order, everything but one or two points and some re-arrangement in the last two chapters.'

It took Michael a minute to recollect that for the past two years he had been at work on the biography of Lord Canning, that two months earlier he had handed John Drexel the manuscript and that for those two months he had got up each morning conscious anew of liberation from his task, a release earned. It was a queer intended vacuum, then, from which every scrap of preoccupation had been evacuated, into which his savage grief had flowed, filling him, he now recognized, with the tension of renewed purpose.

At a quarter to two, over brandy after lunch at John's club, the business of the final chapters discussed over roast beef, he told his publisher he wanted to go to India and that his next work would be about Shivraj.

John treated this announcement with moderate enthusiasm. He believed in distance and detachment in a biographer. Preferably he liked the subject to have been dead a few hundred years. If that were not possible and the subject had more recently trod the earth, he preferred his author not to have known him. Assessment and objectivity were, in his opinion, confused by personal knowledge and attachment. His publishing firm, once his father's, had made a name for itself with, among other things, gems of literary and political biography, and he was something of a connoisseur. He detested with a passion the chatty 'I knew her so well' popular variety, or the stock things American publishers slid like sausage tins across an assembly line, those 'as told to' horrors mouthed by the millionaire's butler and the deodorant magnate's current popsy. Michael was a fine writer but this proposal reeked of involvement. Brooding eyes still swollen with traces of weeping showed more than involvement. Over the years he and Michael had talked about Shivraj, the man, the leader, the friend. This was love, not biographer's ground, and Michael was altogether too tied up with India.

'I think,' said John, tempering his inclination to say no, partly because the glint in Michael's eye was purposeful, a writer's look that came through somehow clear and separate from his grief, 'there can be no harm in waiting.'

'There's no harm in waiting,' repeated Michael slowly. He could not attend Shivraj's funeral, so it did not matter much when after that he got there. 'But it's something I have to do. Good God, John, this was a unique human being, a kind we rarely, if ever, see in politics.'

'We call so many leaders unique,' said John skeptically, 'In what way was Shivraj unique?'

'In the sort of man he was. There was very little about him that was a public image. There's no image-building machinery in India and Indian propaganda is terrible. He was just – himself – and that was what he presented to the public. That was what he gave to policy, as well as to close relationships. Maybe Western policymakers thought him enigmatic because he wore no disguises. They couldn't believe that he, standing there, saying what he did, was all there was. And the Communists, of course, have no use for the contemplative view or vision.'

'You make him sound amazingly simple.'

'Yet he was very complex, as any final simplicity is. It's the end result, isn't it, of so many processes. Shivraj kept arriving at a freshness in looking at things. I have never known another person like that. He insisted on using his mind, not chewed and half-digested bits of other people's.'

'That's why he wrote so well.'

'And so badly,' said Michael with the ghost of a smile, 'ramblingly, the way he spoke. He saw whole vistas and transferred them whole to his writings, as well as when he spoke in public. Yet it worked, as badly constructed novels can become great literature because they contain the breath of life – against all the rules. He *did* convey whole visions and possibilities and get people to work for them.'

John Drexel looked thoughtfully at the wet end of his cigar. There would in due course be the official biography, the birth-to-death tome, with all the material and private papers provided – to someone else. Unless he could persuade the government and Shivraj's family that Michael was the man. Or unless Michael could, with his knowledge of the man and the fingertip sensitivity that was his special gift, extract another kind of story. He was not afraid Michael would exaggerate it in the telling. This excess of grief, this emotional upheaval he was obviously caught in, was insurance that he wouldn't. This was part of the process that would narrow down to the clear stream of judgement when the time came to write.

·Michael refused a lift in John Drexel's taxi, saying he would walk home. He needed an afternoon out-of-doors to clear his head of the rigours of weeping. It reminded him that returning to England ten years earlier had been like coming into a shelter from wind and storm. He had not realized, until he had lived in England again for a while, to what extent the storm had included the passage of each Indian day, how often each day the breaking point was nearly reached in commonplace things like impossible extremes of heat, the overwhelming flavours of food, an unceasing involvement with relationships, the struggle, for him, to understand them, life lived constantly in public. To become even somewhat an Indian was to be caught up in some degree of pandemonium. England in contrast had been unbelievably tranquil, private, placid. That these English – for he could not in the beginning think of them as his own – so civil and so content in their ordinary pursuits and in caring for the things they had built, could ever have ruled half the world, seemed to him quite absurd. That was an occupation for a much more nervous, deluded breed. That they still suffered somewhat from anticlimax was odder still. To Michael it appeared that only now, in the second half of the twentieth century, had they come to the harvest time of their endeavours, the essences they had culled during the thousand years or so – longer than any other people – they had been in charge of their own affairs. It was time to make the most of what really mattered to them, the subtleties they alone in Europe understood, instead of fretting for the finished past or getting tangled in another power formula. This was a time of new opportunity. He felt he was living in England at the proper time, and he had been gradually soothed and restored by the quality this particular race imparted to the air it breathed. He felt connected with the people around him less through blood than pleasant mutual exchange and good will.

His walk took him past the neighbourhood where he had first lived, ten years earlier, and the small unexpected 18th-century church on a street corner not far from his old flat. He had once in curiosity, and often afterward, wandered into it, attracted by its fall of ivy, its ornate wrought-iron enclosed courtyard, everything in and around it in soft summer bloom. He had identified, as he often did, trying to re-learn his surroundings, an oak, a red maple and what the English called bridal wreath. What the English said, did, thought, all had to be discovered slowly again, and birds, flowers and leaves seemed as good a place as any to begin. In the high-vaulted silence of the church, with the day shedding mild milky rays through a big stained glass window, he had spent blank half hours thinking of nothing at all, least of all that for a time life and reason seemed treacherously poised on a knife edge and that it would not matter to future generations which way they tilted, so long as there was no mess for anyone to clean up. And there would not be. His affairs were in impeccable order, from financial arrangements to what was to be done with his body in case of his death, and addresses to be informed. But all of this speculation left him each time he entered the church, as though he had hung it up like a coat at the entrance, not from any habit of religion, but as though this were another, remoter milieu in which these particular details were not relevant. He had entered of choice a seclusion that even friends like John had been reluctant to disturb. Sometimes in those early weeks after his return he had sat in the church not knowing an hour or more had passed, nor that when he left it to walk home, thinking ordinary thoughts again, he was, either way, simply concentrating all his energies on not dying.

He had left India so that he could be, for the first time in several years, an onlooker, an alien, mercifully unentangled with the scene around him, which he could re-learn, tree by tree, street by street, neutrally, Yet today, as he sat at the back of the church, the familiar blankness did not come. Something had crept back under his skin, and his skin crawled with its demands. There was no alternative but to go back to India and meet them. Apart from writing about Shivraj, which was reason enough, ten years was long enough to suspend one's active thoughts about the woman who was his sister. Time, supposed to put everything into perspective, apparently played tricks of another kind with personalities such as his, enlarging and sharpening images. They came back vividly now. He had served his sentence where Devi was concerned, coming away and burying the past, though not, he realized, effectively enough since the two women who had married and divorced him had apparently found his ghosts too tough to contend with.

At home he had put the kettle on for tea when the doorbell rang. It was Nell balancing parcels.

'I've been shopping,' she said.

They had divorced two years earlier but a connection continued. Nell had a healthy resilience that kept her unscarred through crises, and she was sticky about her relationships. She dropped in unasked at intervals for a drink or to make herself a sandwich lunch when she was in town for a visit to the dentist or to see her furniture people. Michael took some of her parcels.

'You look funny, Michael,' she said.

'The Anglo-Saxon male is not permitted to cry. That is why I look funny.'

Nell unloaded herself on to the hall table she had designed, took a comb out of her bag, drew it through her orange hair and joined him in the living room. The morning's papers were all over the floor. One lay spread on the table in the dining alcove.

'What have you been crying about?'

'A man who died.' He indicated the newspapers.

'Oh yes.'

Nell seated herself in a chair by the electric fire, her long yellow-trousered legs crossed, brown roll-topped pullover up to her chin, hair to her shoulders, and lit a cigarette. He marvelled at having married two women so remote in geography and background from the nerve centre of his life. Lydia had thankfully gone her way in a matter of months, leaving him for an oil company executive and disappearing into a world of well-regulated 'seasons' with a wardrobe for each, judging by her appearances in magazines. Her marriage to Michael had disappointed her sorely. She had expected publicity, prestige and a certain amount of well-arranged culture when she married a known author. To her a writer was some kind of public exhibit surrounded by parties, sophisticated chatter and other writers. She had not understood the formidable reality of work, nor that Michael was not more selfish than most people. He was a writer. He had been a medium drinker when he married her.

During Lydia his drinking had blossomed into epic proportion. He was beginning to re-discover England and England was a new elixir, different, changing, vital. The contrast struck him forcefully of great changes gently made, of temperament, climate and countryside exercising a pervasive active calm that held tumult in check. But he couldn't get his hands on any of it during Lydia and it put him in a towering rage. He didn't mind scenes and he made them. He conversed lucidly, brilliantly out loud with himself – because she sat there but would not answer – searching for clues to England, trying to understand its challenges, its future. Their future after all, and their country. A thousand pounds had been spent on making Lydia a lady, and she sat knees and ankles together, every hair in place, being a lady, with no comment. She was prepared to discuss things with him, she said in her dignified way, when he wasn't 'drunk'. As it turned out that was almost never but in any case Lydia had no use for the abstract. It bored her. His vague hope that he might carry Lydia with him to some creative excess faded out. So did his epic drinking when she left him. They had both been relieved when it ended, though it had left a blank unanswered in his own mind about himself. And again with Nell, whose departure he had regretted.

'That's the whistle,' said Nell, 'I'll go and make tea.'

She brought the tray back into the room.

'Of course you knew him very well, didn't you, Michael? D'you think the bond between men friends is somehow truer?'

Nell was young and talked young, and it became her.

'There's an Arab saying to that effect. I can't remember how it goes.'

'That's different. They have no use for women except as women. Nor do you. You go on using them up like matches because the right one wouldn't have you years ago.'

Michael dismissed the idea.

'I don't get through women. They get through me. Lydia walked out. So did you.'

'Because it's not self-respecting being married to you, Michael.' said Nell good-naturedly, 'though you're nice to know otherwise.'

'I like your orange hair,' he said irrelevantly. The twin bars of the electric heater gave it a fiery glow. She reminded him of fresh sun-ripened fruit.

'It's auburn, thank you very much.'

'The skin of a Spanish orange,' insisted Michael, 'and you look delectable in those colours. How is the furniture business?'

Nell blushed. 'It's all right. Quite good, actually. I'm making money.'

'I had a talk with John Drexel today. I'm going to India later this year.'

'What a good idea,' said Nell unexpectedly, 'Then you've finished Canning?'

For the second time that day he felt exposed, an inner skin showing without a book to retreat into. Wonderful how a book insulated you. He wouldn't have noticed Nell's hair or the bloom on her cheeks if he'd been immersed in Canning. One went around blind and unnoticing. He would have to start work on the Shivraj book soon. He now found the pauses between his various writing assignments trying. They brought him too sharply up against ordinary human contact. He was used to living mostly with the dead he wrote about.

'I'm planning a book about Shivraj,' he said, 'I'm sorry there's nothing to eat.' He remembered she liked to munch something with tea or a drink.

'It doesn't matter. Before you start the new book let's spend an evening together. What about week after next? I have to be in town again on the 21st.'

Michael found a canvas bag to hold all her parcels, saw her down the stairs and opened the heavy front door for her. She had a mole at the corner of her mouth and her hair was smooth and straight on both sides of her centre parting. With Nell there had been good possibilities. He thought about them as he went up the stairs. He had lived half a life these ten years, except for his writing.

When Devi opened her eyes her first drowsy thought was that she had nothing suitable to wear to the party she was attending that night, or to any coming social event, and that it might be weeks before she could go shopping to her heart's content. Looking at fashion magazines before falling asleep was a mistake. In any case they never had clothes for engagements like hers, Cabinet meetings, public appearances and tours, and it was time Indian designers devised a next-to-nothing garment, instead of yards and yards of sari, to keep a working woman cool, sane and efficient in this dementing heat. She closed her eyes and her thoughts scattered far and wide, dreaming of paradise – the garden at home when the rains came, distilling magic fragrances from the soft drowned earth. The chemistry, the poetry, the majesty of the rains! No other season had counted as much with her. She had run out enraptured to dance and play in the first downpour like a pagan or a savage, like the earliest human ever to welcome its great orchestral fanfare on the Gangetic plain. Did everyone's childhood seem such a lifetime away? She woke up every morning thinking of rain. Rain in January clearing the air to an unbelievable radiance. Unexpected rain the day long ago when Shivraj, impatiently putting aside the umbrella offered to him on the dais, had spoken, drenched, to the huge wet unmoving gathering of women, and Devi had ecstatically pledged, mixing up her life with his, 'I'll follow you to the ends of the earth,' while rain plastered her hair and clothes against her. The organizing years when women had been trained and sent into villages and district towns had been partly her effort.

The alarm beside her bed rang, rousing her again. Six a.m. The beginning of a new day, or with the monsoon holding evilly off, like the continuation of the previous day, or even the one before that, a stale sagging weary accumulation of more hours than any single day should have to bear; a load that did not disappear into the night to make room for a new day, but dragged on until finally it lay dying of its own exhaustion. So the new day could begin at sunset, with an unexpected breeze, the first stir of any living thing in a week; or when it was nearly night and momentarily a whisper of rain hung shyly about, mingling with the sound of bells from the Sikh gurdwara down the road. Or, if she were up to see it, in the pale coral sky of very early morning.

This particular day she could tell, though the air-conditioner was on, was still the old one, and the temperature out and indoors, though different, would not feel much so. It had been a tiring August, weather that made one think of one's age, of time gone. While Shivraj had lived she had thought of the years ahead as being many and varied, a glowing mature time to come, when things not necessarily visible or tangible would bear fruit. She and Shivraj would grow old together – as she and Ishwar had never been allowed to. They would read books there had been no time for, listen for hours to music, make a garden, enjoy Rishad in his man-hood and then Rishad's children. Now the future, on a mid-week morning like this, was just whatever time was left. And at forty-four she wondered how much and what kind that was. She was at the age when according to the magazines women in the West lost their husbands to young girls. Suddenly her natural impatience asserted itself. She knew she was not about to be abandoned by any-thing, least of all her optimism. She was in a position of command. Though she suspected they had made her Education Minister because, in the emotional aftermath of Shivraj's death, they could not very well ignore her. In the next Cabinet reshuffle, or on some pretext they would dispense with her. They hadn't known, when they asked her to join – though how it could have escaped them was ironic – that she had a mind of her own and in a position of authority she would use it. Wasn't that what authority was for? She hadn't known when she accepted, that she would need to quite so much. But the curious guidelines she received from them left her no alternative. These were men who had never, by the looks of it, done anything with their hands, or had any collision with real life. It struck her forcefully for the first time that this particular group of 'intellectuals' might never have come to power at all if Shivraj had lived to his normal span. Shivraj had been fond of them, consulted with them on occasions, and firmly ruled them out as mature partners in government. They were attractive, intense and ungrown – as was anyone who could seriously believe that one hypothesis, unshakeable, unquestionable, could be true for all time. And now here they were, trying to make a revolution by the rules of a book, while the class war they had blithely begun simmered in the streets outside their offices, and they apparently had not a practical notion in their professorial heads what to do about it. Except throw it more bait, more scraps of raw red meat from time to time, in the form of good rabble-rousing speeches and lavish promises. Then they were surprised the rabble had been roused, and that in the sweltering August heat of Delhi, in the streets and bazaars and power plants, in the corridors of the university and at the railway station, things were happening that they could no longer control.

Devi had been waiting as though for a signal, and it came. The air conditioner's audible hum rose to a rattle, grated harshly and stopped, and the silence became what it so rarely was, completely soundless, with not just the small murmurs of living, but everything sword-cut at a stroke. She had a moment of panic: when we are very old it will still be like this, nothing changed, nothing better. Shivraj's successors, playing at revolution, have set the clock back dangerously. All the sovereign forces that bring change and improvement and mellowness in the course of time have been cut off like that air conditioner. Perhaps deliberately. Almost as if there were an intelligence at work and its design included large soggy pieces of failure, one contaminating another like monsoon fungus. The air conditioner gutturally stopping, as though at a signal, happened often enough. And suppose something were, this time, mechanically wrong with it, an electrician might or might not turn up to repair it, if she were an ordinary citizen and not a Minister, that is. Her own would be attended to. For others it would depend on law and order where the electrician lived, and whether he felt like coming or not. Too much depended on too many people outside oneself. It always had, but one noticed it now that the interconnected reliability upon which daily life rested had disappeared.

Moist heat materialized, a limp damp presence in the room, and Devi pushed aside the sheet covering her to get up and open the windows. With the air-conditioner off, household sounds came to her clearly, including the ring of the telephone in the small front office where Ram Murti, her chief P.A., who must have just arrived, was answering it. She could not hear him but she knew he was saying the Minister was in the bathroom. Her callers between six and eight a.m. were invariably told she was in the bathroom, unless it was urgent, when he sent for her. Ram Murti was an experienced sifter of calls and staver off of time-wasters. He had worked in the Secretariat for ten years, had quickly recognized her inexperience, and had devised ways to conserve her energies. He understood a populist democracy rather as a rough ocean banging the rocks at its edge and reducing them at times to sliding gravel. The public was unrelenting in its demands on the Minister. He had watched Ministers come and go, seen the politically sure ones resist pressures and come out smooth and undented. They could face question hour in Parliament, address public meetings, handle the cavalcade of humanity that paraded through a Minister's day and even thrive on all the commotion. But there were the raw ones who, if conscientious, got worn away like so much sand. Ram Murti had not known where to place Devi at first. She had considerable knowledge of the countryside, and had had charge for years of the women's wing of the Party, but she had never been a Minister. Within two weeks of her assuming office he had sized her up and decided he must look out for important calls and firmly bar the trivial. All this without ever actually looking her in the face. She wondered if Ram Murti even knew what she looked like.

Devi had a bath and dressed, looking out as she did at the small oval lawn that was her garden. She had not taken a Minister's bungalow. What would she and Rishad have done with a big house and spreading lawns? The globe lights signifying a Minister's residence had had to be put onto her gates. When she went into the dining room for her breakfast of brown bread and coffee, Rishad was already at the table, looking tired and sleepy. He did most of his studying at night. Devi rumpled his hair, kissed his cheek and sat down.

'My air-conditioner went off again this morning,' she told him.

Rishad made a sympathetic noise through his mouthful of toast. Then he swallowed it and said, 'Actually, Mum, so few people *have* air-conditioners. It's not a problem most people face.'

Younger version of professorial evasion at Cabinet meetings. She considered saying that even if there were only one air-conditioner on the entire peninsula, it should be one that worked. As it happened, there were thousands. Offices were using them. So were private houses, and industries were manufacturing them. They cost thousands of rupees to buy and were expensive to run. So why on earth shouldn't they be expected to work? She didn't say it because she felt tender toward the instincts that prompted his views. He was nineteen, not fifty, and his dreams had time to grow sound working muscle. For the professors it was already too late.

She said, instead, 'But lots more people use lights and fans and trains, and they keep stopping too.'

Rishad started to say something. He looked at his intelligent mother measuringly and kept quiet. Devi saw the look. Rishad's control and containment worried her. Men took years to arrive at it. Rishad at nineteen was there already and she wondered what he had missed along the way. It was so unusual in one so young; out of keeping, too, with his generation, and so pronounced that it took people much longer to notice anything else about him, the critical brilliance that made him an outstanding student, the fine-grained sensitivity he could talk with when the spirit moved him. Caught between ancient myth and industrial present, it was no wonder if any young or even older person found life a little bewildering. Not that this one did. Rishad was cool and sure, quiet and courteous. He was intent on his studies, a strong candidate for a coveted scholarship to higher studies abroad after his degree. He was that rarity, a real student. His saving grace, if he ever needed one, was his love for his work. If he had any unpalatable views, his mother had never heard them. He neither agreed nor disagreed vehemently with what was said in the house. He was perhaps simply 'against' whatever there was, not a bad position at nineteen. Though again, in Rishad, not enough either. The boy had lived too close to the bone of high aspiration and endeavour since his birth to be quite so non-committal.

Ram Murti came into the dining room and told the coffee pot that the Vice-Chancellor was on the telephone. He wanted to know if he could postpone his interview with her to the afternoon as he was required at the university all morning. Devi decided that she would go and see him at the university instead. 'And please come back and have a cup of coffee, Ram Murti.' She knew he would say, 'No thank you, Madam. I have already had some in my office,' where Kirti, her cook, looking like thunder must have served it to him. But before many more days had passed she intended to make Ram Murti sit down and have a cup of coffee *with* her at the table. If for no other reason than that she must repay him for his many services and the patience with which he dealt with her ignorance of official matters.

Rishad said, 'I won't be home for lunch, Mum. I'm going to spend the afternoon in the library.'

'Nor will I.'

During the monsoon or the no-monsoon session, as it was turning out, of Parliament, she took lunch with her to office and today she had an appointment very near lunch time.

'What are you going to see the Vice Chancellor about?' asked Rishad.

Devi's hand with its piece of bread stopped midway to her mouth.

'What about?' she repeated in surprise.

'Oh, the demonstration yesterday,' said Rishad.

The demonstration yesterday had flared like a fierce brief fire, leaving charred remains around it. Like dry timber, forests of it, ready for a careless match, the universities waited, and small and big fires raged. They had needed all her energy and ingenuity since she had taken office, to put out. And they never quite went out. The smoke never cleared. The sickness was too deep. Till recently Delhi University had been free from trouble but what had made her think the capital was immune?

'Can you tell me something about it?' she asked her son.

'All we know is Uncle Usman expelled the three students who raped the girl, and there was a demonstration against him. It got pretty wild. I think he got hurt.'

'What were they demonstrating about ? Supporting the rape?'

'No of course not. They were protesting against the expulsion of the three students. It's hard enough to get a job with a degree, and without one it's impossible.'

Devi waited for him to say something about the girl. The trouble with principles and theories, even perfect ones, was that they dealt with people in the mass. She felt acutely the plight of the jobless young, but a boiling rage filled her at the barbarism of rape on campus, a helpless young girl probably injured for life. The wrong way round obviously. According to the book rules 'the mass' should have had her sympathy first. She looked down at the folded newspaper near her plate, her favourite political cartoon figure, Mansa Ram, on the front page. Mansa Ram believed it was a good world if your rulers were good. All the rest could be borne. The bus lumbered away loaded to bursting, leaving him standing on the pavement with a crowd of others. The others gesticulated angrily and shook their fists but Mansa Ram stood patient and puzzled. He had been marched off more than once in processions to demonstrate about something, a placard on a pole thrust into his hand, he looking up at it with great goodwill and bewilderment. This morning he was staring fascinatedly at the municipal tap in his neighbourhood watching the next drop of water appear, lazily swell and plop into his bucket as though his vigil would help it to gush, while his neighbours, brisk and practical, went off abandoning all hope of water. Mansa Ram's jog-trot existence had been funny enough but lately his creator had been having trouble visualizing him. Mansa Ram was becoming sad. There were things happening around him he could no longer understand. Soon he might become a figure of tragedy with no place in a comic strip. Perhaps the newspaper would start a tragic strip.

'What's happening to Mansa Ram today?' asked Rishad.

Devi passed him the newspaper.

'I wish he'd become less of a victim. He should take the initiative about something.'

'About what, for instance?'

'Well, *demand* something, act as if he knew what he were about.'

'He isn't about anything, except living his own quiet life. The others around him are the demanders.'

'I'm tired of his looking so bewildered.'

'He wouldn't be funny if he didn't,' said Devi.

'Yes, I see. But it isn't very funny to go through some of the things he goes through.'

'No, but that's the message, the pathos, the other side of laughter.

A cartoon isn't an essay.' Or dialectics, she was tempted to add, and short of going mad, what else was there at times but laughter?

Six constituents waiting on her verandah for her to finish breakfast greeted her as she came out. From contracts to heartache a good deal of business got enacted before she left the house. Appointments like so much else were a luxury confined to countries with populations of fifty not five hundred million, and neat small educated Parliaments. She had seen each day swallow Shivraj up in an avalanche of people and problems, apart from his desk work. Now she knew this was the normal flow and gush of political life and that anyone serving India had to leave his personal life behind him.

Three hours later she left her office at Shastri Bhavan to drive past the broken outer wall of the Purana Quila in its stone sleep of centuries under the sun, toward the old city, thinking that lately she and Usman Ali had met only to discuss how to plug explosions. He had been one of Shivraj's dearest friends and remained hers. It was he who had given Rishad his Muslim name. Since her entry into the Cabinet she had turned to him more and more for his advice. Shown into the Vice Chancellor's office she stopped, catching her breath on the threshold as Usman Ali came forward to greet her with an embrace.

'I left it like this,' he apologized, 'to give you an idea of what happened yesterday, since you insisted on coming yourself. Now we'll go and sit in another room.'

She said stupidly, 'Usman, are you badly hurt?'

He saw the shock in her face. 'I thought you'd have read about me. It was in the morning papers.'

She shook her head.

'It probably looks worse than it is. A flying splinter caught my eye. I have to keep it bandaged. The doctor will look at it again today.'

She gestured toward his arm-sling. It had broken in two places, he admitted. He did not mention that his hip had also been hurt.

'Let's go,' he urged.

'No, let's stay here.' The room was part of the reality that had to be faced.

'But, my dear, there's nowhere to sit.'

Agitatedly, she picked up a chair and tried to set it on its legs. It wobbled, one leg shorter than the others. None of the other few items of furniture looked all in one piece either. They had, Usman told her, hurled stones through the window to start with, but later they had stormed into the building through the front door to finish the job. He took her to a room down the corridor whose smallness had escaped notice. It was the first time that a visit from Devi had been so overshadowed by the occasion of it but he was determined to salvage what pleasure he could from their meeting. Usman, whose explorations of the past had included a study of the Indian woman from Vedic times never knew quite how to classify Devi. From where, in the long saga, did she derive her particular qualities? Possibly right at the start. There was an air of beginnings about her, of discovery, a transparency that had never grown any tough outer crust. Her animation was not of talk or gesture. It radiated from within, through her skin and her eyes, from the source of her being. She was a golden creature, composed of layers of light, and light invaded places. Neither her looks nor her intellect was exceptional. What she possessed was some luminous persistent quality of life, a refusal not to flourish. And with all this she was so delightfully adult. His affectionate name for her was Shahbano, Persian for the King's Consort, to which she objected strenuously. Shivraj was not a king and this was no kingdom, but a republic. He could look at her when she said that, with his keen assessing grey eyes and reply quite accurately, 'But we're nostalgic for kings, or charismatic leaders, or some shining example that stands out from the millions, republic though we might be. Five thousand years of memories and attachments don't vanish at the sound of three syllables.'

She was sitting there now looking appalled and shaken.

'Something cold for you to drink, Shahbano?'

She declined, smiling at the name, but said in a low voice, 'God, Usman, they could have put your eye out. They could have killed you.'

He said with a trace of weariness, 'The point is "they" is now ourselves. Our own. Our children. And this mess will never be sorted out as long as we keep sprouting new universities. No less than five new ones are being set up in the northeast. Universities can't be scattered like birdseed. It isn't possible to deal in ideas until we become much more selective, and we can't do that if every job requires a degree.'

They had been over it half a dozen times already, turning the main problem over between them, here on his ground, or in his study at home, or at her house. They had talked for hours, and he had had hours of discussion with chosen members of the faculty. He had also spent some months preparing a document for her Ministry on the need for reform and the manner in which it might be brought about.

Devi said thoughtfully, 'My colleagues keep saying there was not enough change in Shivraj's time.'

'Where do your colleagues live, Shahbano? From the bullock cart to supersonic jet aircraft, hundreds of dams and canals, electrification for miles of village countryside, is quite a change, Even your colleagues must realize we've travelled some distance. The problems on our hands are the problems of change. And nowhere has it been so unwieldy as in education.'

'I need your help, Usman.'

'You have it, and we have to act without delay. But I shall need yours, too. We won't go into all that now,' he said in answer to the enquiry in her eyes, 'Later sometime.'

'What about the poor little girl' she asked.

He gave her the details he had.

'We've been able to make no clear headway with our investigation. All our information has been picked up at random from students. The three responsible for the outrage have not been caught yet. The girl's parents won't see or talk to anyone. They don't want more publicity for what is already an intolerable disgrace.'

'I'll go myself to see them.'

'That may help.'

'What possessed those three to behave so monstrously?'

Usman said, 'They are in no way representative of the student body.'

'Nor, I suppose, were those who assaulted you yesterday.'

'Devi, there are about sixty thousand at this university. Yesterday's mob was not more than forty or fifty.'

Usman, a scholar, humorous, patient, compassionate, had all the qualities that had once been considered enough to preside successfully over a student community. What else was required now?

He saw her out to her car and Ajaib Singh, her chauffeur, saluted him smartly. Once of the army, Ajaib Singh still looked a soldier. He also looked the farmer he was, with a self-confidence not found in the city-bred. And his sheer size made him difficult to ignore. The security man looked quite puny next to him.

'You will go back to office now, Sir?'

Devi's domestic staff called her Bibiji, but for Ajaib Singh she was Sir, a recognition of equality from him. He knew the security man had to come along but he believed him to be superfluous when he, Ajaib Singh, stood like a solid wall between Sir and anyone who might have the temerity to try and harm a hair of her head. He had no personal loyalty to her. She was simply his employer, and of course, Shivraj's sister. Devi gave him the address in the bazaar Usman Ali had given her of Madhu's home.

'This is hardly the time to buy sweets. Only the leftovers will be there now,' said Ajaib Singh.

The security man, conscious of status and protocol, looked uncomfortable and nudged Ajaib Singh, whose superior he felt he was, to get going.

Devi retorted, 'We're not going to buy sweets – heaven forbid in this heat – and you haven't made any auspicious announcement that I know of – we're going to see someone there.'

Ajaib Singh chuckled. He liked her. She could crack a joke or two, heat or no heat. The security fellow, dying of protocol, he noticed, was busy trying to hide his smile under his moustache instead of letting it show. Not that that moustache would hide anything, let alone that feeble excuse for a smile.

Nearly an hour later Devi emerged from the lane where Madhu's home was, from the smell of old grease, refuse and decay surrounding it, with Madhu and her sister-in-law beside her. The woman, her sari pulled low over her face, said nothing all the way to the hospital. The girl's replies to Devi's quiet inconsequential talk were muttered, but at least she no longer lay disintegrating under shock as she had looked when Devi found her on her bed, staring at the ceiling, fortunately out of earshot of the despairing family council in the courtyard. Devi stole a look at the blunt profile with its short upturned nose, at the stubby small hands bunched into fists on her lap, and felt immensely relieved at the outcome of her visit. We might be instruments of a process as the Cabinet professors keep saying, but the process is not the State or anonymous brotherhood, it's our love for our children, and through them all others.

When she got home from office at six that evening she hoped it was not too late to remind Rishad about the party they had both been invited to. Fortunately he was home.

'Rishi, I hope you're coming to Pinky's engagement party.'

'What in the world will I do there? Besides, that kind of marriage is just organized rape.' One way or another the hideous word kept figuring in her day. 'Pinky hasn't been allowed to put her nose out of the house without her mother's permission. And now they're handing her over like a pudding to that nitwit who hasn't put his nose out of his house – his mental nose anyway. Talk about rape at the university. I think this is quite obscene.'

'Anyway their noses seem perfectly matched,' mumbled Devi, glancing through the letters lying on the hall table and leaving them there, 'Rishi, why can't you just come? Everything's not a matter of principle. And you've known her all your life.'

Rishad put loving arms around his mother. 'I can't possibly come,' he said with finality.

We have our line of battle, and neither crosses. I don't myself, she admitted, recalling the day she was to take her Ministerial oath of office and Rishad asking her at breakfast, 'Are you going to swear by God or solemnly affirm?' 'Swear by God', she told him. 'How could you? An educated woman, in this day and age.' It was a hard one to answer in points one two and three, involving more living and feeling than Rishad yet had to his credit, and he was not the man to take anything on trust meanwhile. She did not blame him. She had not taken things on trust either at his age. She had that morning as usual stayed peaceably on her side of the line – and sworn by God at the oath-taking. No other Minister had.

3

After he had seen Devi off, Usman Ali went back into his office. He switched on the fan. Its swift-moving blades blew dust and shredded paper across a scene of unfamiliar chaos. But its thread of singing sound brought back memories of harmony, blazing summer afternoons spent in cool rooms, blinds down, the ceiling fan between humanity and the heat. Once an unobtrusive, thus-far-and-no-further science had stood between comfort and discomfort, pain and relief, heat and cool. Many people had done even without that. And they, the millions, had looked incongruous, not when fierce heat battered the ancient plain, but during the brief winter, faces muffled to the nose, shawl-enwrapped against the cold. The heat was their normal temperature, their climate, their natural world. They managed it in little ways. They moved in it and with it, not in great wasteful onslaughts against it.

Usman looked round the room, caught in the persistent low fever of things that needed puzzling out. With his left arm he picked up the chair Devi had tried to set on its legs and turned it over to examine the damage, trying to picture the kind of heavy blunt instrument that would leave it in just that state of imbalance. He was beginning to think they had come rehearsed to produce this handiwork, not wrecked the room in spontaneous anger against his expulsion of three students. Did they, then, before they gathered for the demonstration, pick and choose the instruments they would bring with them, this to smash with, that for more detailed destruction? The chair he held had seen better days and had not required much force to dismember. But the upholstered sofa and matching chair, dilapidated though they were, had taken time and thoroughness to gouge out. And time was the element incompatible to him with destruction. Yet nowadays, unlike any age past, people actually took time to destroy, deliberately made this very bizarre use of time. Surely this was the only era in history when what had gone before had been earmarked for demolition to make room for change. In other ages men had built on what they already had, made changes from where they took over. No one had wanted to wipe out the previous human record. But for the current crop of interpreters, nothing apparently grew. It sprang formidably full-grown from the head of chaos. This debris, this mangled confetti were its symbols. Destroy – and ye shall find.

They thought of the past as a monolith to seize and destroy. From long experience as a teacher he knew it could not be destroyed. Sooner or later it flowed back, and in spite of its accusers, it did not prevent people from learning new things. A new *technique* particularly made no demands on the spirit, betrayed no gods. Usman had been a Communist in his youth, determined to wipe out the old gods, but he had changed. The only kind of Communism he could have accepted was a native Indian Communism with its roots in the village and its inspiration drawn from the Indian heritage. But that was not the kind India had. He had come to believe over the years that the hammer and sickle, symbols of respect and resurgence, were only two of the tools the new society would need. Every tool and every class that wielded it would count, the educated as much as the mass. He went to the steel cupboard and unlocked it, thankful to find his files and his bulky document on education, his 'blueprint' as Devi incorrectly called it – it was nothing so defined as that – safely intact. The revolutionary things in India had seldom been accomplished with fanfare. This, the disbanding of most universities, would be one of them. Upon it a new concept of education would arise.

Drawers had been pulled out of his desk, their contents flung all over the room. Faces he saw at assembly, fingers that transcribed notes to paper, heads bent over volumes in the library had conceived and delivered this spectacle. They were making war. What on, apart from the expulsions he had announced? He should know, heading an institution that was becoming a battlefield. And he felt ill-equipped to know, belonging to a generation nurtured on the belief that life's most productive possibilities lay between extremes. Only forty or fifty, he had told Devi, had been responsible for this violence. But when had it taken more than forty or fifty to engineer destruction? And how would he deal with this attack or prevent another? What precisely was he up against. A shiver of fear travelled up his spine. He had come close to being killed, and one of these days he might get killed for no particular reason. Perhaps for believing that this was a land and a people whose ultimate flowering would be one of the kindlier chapters of civilization. Though now that did not seem so inevitable. Less and less since yesterday. Accustomed to the disorders of student gatherings, yesterday for the first time he had seen cold indifference deal out vicious fury, an unnatural alliance terrifying in its implications. Usman could understand personal violence. It even helped sometimes to clear the atmosphere. Hot fury spent itself. But this would not. It would happen again and again. He felt ridiculously unsafe.

On a day like this he missed Shivraj. Shivraj had had the gift of putting things in perspective, and since his death Usman had become convinced that that was leadership's main task. To put into perspective. To gather up the facts and fevers and strands, the achievement and the discouragement, and place it where it could be seen against the whole, the past, the future. To assemble the broken fragments and light up their possibilities. To tell the cripple, Take up thy bed and walk. To resurrect the dead. Leadership did not join the ferment, scream with the mob. Leadership led. Funny, it was not Shivraj's enemies who were undoing what he had done. It was his friends, his following, those who had written paeans of praise to him. Strange that the individuality, the diversity of India had been congealed by these, the poets and heralds of freedom and the new dawn, the avant-garde, into a glutinous mass of verbiage that abounded in clichés. A nation accustomed to Shivraj's thinking, and Shivraj's vocabulary, reduced to *this*? The world had gone too far, it had gone quite mad, in this cult of elaborate concern with its lack of true practical concern. It would have to desert the mob and come back soon to the individual. Devi's face, the anxiety in her eyes, eyes that had lost none of their brilliance since he had first known her, came back to him, a reminder of more than friendship with her and with Shivraj. He felt a peculiar grief at the memory of the man, not at his death, untimely though it had been, but at the passing with him of some vital human essence.

Devi's husband he had known much less well, and he had seen little of Devi during her few married years. It must have been three months or so after Ishwar's death that he had called, after a long interval, at her house. The relatives who had filled the house, the people who had been coming and going for weeks, had gone and Shivraj had taken a train to Bombay that afternoon. Usman calling out Devi's name had received no answer and he felt he crossed great empty expanses in the short distance to her room, uncannily in tune with the desolation she must be feeling. She had been lying face downward on her bed, one arm flung out on the bed next to hers. He had gently lifted that arm, lain down and taken Devi in his arms, wanting to comfort and protect her. He had known Devi as a brain, an ability, an attractiveness. He had often, disinterestedly, noted the loveliest line of her body, her slim indented waist, but he had not truly known her till that evening. The act of love had never been so simple, fulfilling an unconscious yearning in himself to know her better, deeply, as alone a man and a woman can know each other. And he knew beyond any doubt that the feel of her breasts under his hand and his seeking mouth, was in some way setting her free. She would not end her abundant emotional life at Ishwar's pyre. She would live, and more. He had helped to restore that lovely pride, the assurance and aristocracy of her. She had wept a little in his arms but then they had sat for a long while talking, not touching each other, Devi of the experience she could hardly bear to remember, the sight of the body she had loved in flames. Was burial better, Usman had asked? Death, however we dealt with it, was so final. Yet he could understand her horror of cremation. It took a special grit to watch a disposal so awesomely enacted before one's eyes. Talking to him about it seemed to deliver her from that spectacle too. By common consent, their love-making had rarely gone as far as that again, though Usman had made love to her in small, satisfying ways, and now for a long time not even that. Usman went behind his desk again and picked up the telephone — they had fortunately forgotten to cut the wire — to tell his wife he would stop off at Dr. Jaipal's clinic before coming home. A servant answered and Usman spoke to him.

As he replaced the telephone, he instinctively moved out from behind his desk as though it had become a barricade, an obstruction to understanding what went on on the other side. Some of yesterday's faces sprang into his vision. He clearly recalled one of them, sharp and bitter, a thin face on a hollowed neck, with more than anger against a Vice Chancellor branded into it. And Usman with dawning astonishment realized that for this face and the others he represented authority sheltering behind the status quo, lacking in gentleness and understanding of them. That was not the side he belonged to at all. He had come out from established positions all his life, stepping into the unkown with complete conviction. Years earlier he had walked out of academic life at another university where he was beginning to acquire a brilliant reputation, to join the national movement and go to jail. He had done it again when he had returned his Communist party card to follow another leader. Revolutions, if they had any meaning, meant putting oneself into the crucible of change. Revolutions went on. They did not get congealed in their tracks or follow beaten tracks. And people who loved as he did, the past, the present and the future of their country, had to be willing to change.

Madhu had not known she was shouting until the nurse bent down and clamped her hand hard over her mouth and held it there till she stopped. 'You're disturbing the whole ward. What are you shouting about? It's finished.' Madhu opened her eyes. She lay on a mattress on the floor near the end of the long room. Other mattresses lay to her left and hospital beds stretched away to her right. She could see the rows of iron legs. the iron webbing underneath the one nearest her. She had no pain now but ragged sobs kept rising in her chest and escaping in cries she did not know she was uttering. She had received a message that she should go to the registrar's office but when she got there it was empty. She heard a key turn in the lock and the three of them stood in the room, one with a beard and two without. One of the clean-shaven ones pushed her down on the floor. She fell hitting her head on a corner of the desk and it stunned her. A torturing pain had gone through her in ways she could not recognize. She had screamed and felt the froth rising to her lips before they had gagged her. It was the bearded one who unlocked the door and ran before his turn came, sending the other two after him. The nurse bent over her again. 'Enough, d'you hear? I've got other things to do.' The nurse kept saying it was finished but it wasn't. The bearded one would be back later, alone.

They sent her home from the hospital in the evening. Past the cloth that served as a curtain, hung carelessly over the bent curtain rod between the courtyard and the room she shared with her younger sisters, she could see her sister-in-law squatting at the tap, trying to scrub utensils under its slow sucking drip. She heard her elder brother return from his shop in the bazaar and the street sounds outside – noises of argument and trundling traffic, children's shrill games and mongrels yelping – dissolve to a more subdued evening tempo. String cots were dragged into the courtyard for the family to sit on and she shut her ears to their talk because it was about her. She shut her eyes. The key turned in the lock and the three of them stood in the room. Now she saw them in more detail. The first one had a pen clipped to his pocket. His hair was longer than the second one's. The one with the beard had a hand in his pocket. With the key, Madhu began to shout.

'Nadira?' Instinct impelled Usman toward the bedroom instead of the study where he had hoped to have a late quiet cup of tea. She must have had hers by now. Nadira was lying on her bed, the shades down, her lilac-scented cologne in the air.

'Do you have a headache?'

'I'll get up,' she said.

'Don't get up if you have a headache.' He stood at the end of her bed.

Nadira sat up, looked at him, covered her face with her hands and began to sob. Usman went to the windows for something to do, and raised the shades. They had been through all this yesterday.

'What have they done to you? They're going to kill you. They're after you because you're a Muslim.'

'That's rubbish,' he said evenly. He secured each window shade with care. It took time with only one hand. 'I'll order tea.'

'I want to get away. It's getting on my nerves. I'm going to stay with my family in Lahore.'

In May he had suggested her going to the hills with the children, but she had sent the children away with friends and had not gone.

'Yes, do. Take the children. It won't matter if they miss a little of school. And the change will do you good.'

It was not what she wanted to hear. He had not acknowledged the reason for her wanting to go. Her religious narrowness had been something of a shock to him. He had never imagined such a possibility. Of the many-roomed mansion of Islam, its language, its art and architecture, its scholarship and brotherhood and piety, she had chosen to dwell spiritually in the blind alley that ran past it, the dark breeding ground of superstition. In this country, at this time, her lament had a mournful medieval clangour about it, a refusal to focus on reality.

He left the room to order tea, switched on the living room fan and sat down, his mind in a turmoil over yesterday's happenings, and the tense months before that of his Vice-Chancellorship. His eye throbbed with pain and though the doctor had said it would heal he wondered if his sight had been affected. He put a hand over his bandaged eye, in an effort to stop the throbbing and went over the queer catalogue of the week's events. On Monday, he had received a student delegation demanding that those who had failed to obtain a degree in the May examination be allowed to sit for it again. On Tuesday a group of students had captured a bus and burned it on campus. The bus had been full and the driver had tried to prevent the students from boarding it. He was, Usman hoped, in hospital recovering from a beating and severe burns. On Wednesday the girl had been raped and a rash of violence had erupted in several colleges of the university. On Friday his office and others had been invaded and ransacked and he had been assaulted. So had three other members of the faculty who had been in their offices at the time. The damage at other colleges had yet to be assessed. On Saturday, today, he had declared the university closed. Where did he go from there?

Nadira came in, her long dark hair tied back with a ribbon, tendrils of it escaping. Her thick-lashed eyes had the tragic drenched look crying gave her. Crying suited her. It went with the langour she could cultivate so appealingly. During the first year or two of their marriage, before their attitudes had hardened, she had charmed his friends with her romantic looks, studied manners and her slight but promising poetic talent. But soon she had gone into a kind of mourning, a reflection on him, on his country and the creed he lived by. She would not come to meet him on religion. She would not discuss it rationally. He guessed she wanted a dire enough confrontation on it that would turn him to her way of

32

thinking, make him admit she was right. According to her, this was it and she would not see it otherwise, as part of a surge that had to do with almost everything that was wrong in the country, and nothing to do with religion. Somewhere, her antagonisms were all connected, too, with the personal. He could still admire her physical perfection, the length of her limbs, each separate visual offering. She was a woman to make love to by daylight, to linger over in bed, and have nothing whatever to do with for the rest of the twenty-four hours. If one were compartmentally made. He was not. He had married late and never worried about the gap between their ages. His friends had told him it was a risk. She was much too young for him and one of these days another man would be more attractive to her. It had not happened. Usman had a quality that made women cling. Nadira had become obsessional about him. When he left the house each morning he assumed she must have a life of her own. But he could not picture it. In his presence she refused to let anything else matter to her.

The servant brought tea and Nadira poured out some for herself too.

'I waited for you,' she said, a broken brittle edge to her voice, 'I'm always waiting for you.'

She meant bed. He calculated how long it had been since he had slept with her. About ten days. He had made a note in his diary about it. He had started keeping a note so that he did not neglect her for long periods. He didn't know whether this matter-of-factness was cruelty or compassion. Fulfilling this responsibility meticulously made him less guilty about the absolute privacy he needed more and more.

'I won't go to Lahore. I want to be with you.' she said.

Be with. Yet she was not with him in his friendships and loyalties, in the passions of his mind and heart, in his central concerns. When he took a woman he took a mind as well. He had no use for just bodies. Every woman he had intimately known had been incomparably more to him than that. It was the final irony that this had not happened with his own wife. She remained so determinedly a body.

'You don't get time to talk to me any more. I wonder if you even see me.'

Usman took her hand. His solicitude was genuine. He wished they could share this crisis together, but he knew it was not possible. Brutality, which he preferred in argument, produced only tears. He had stopped arguing. He abandoned the interlude he had planned in his study. With his eye hurting and the difficulty of holding a pen, it would be a waste of time anyway. He sorted out what to say and what not to say to Nadira for the next quarter hour until he could with reasonable courtesy slip out of the house for a walk. He decided he would make love to her that night though it would be awkward with his right arm out of commission. With Nadira the inveighing and enticing, the ebb and flow of courtship continued. There had once been an excitement about it. There still was when she was relaxed. She was durable as mistress material, problematic as a wife. She did not settle down. His enjoyment of her had to consist of what she would willingly give him, and that remained within the ambit of their physical relationship.

4

The day was not yet over. Devi went into the kitchen to tell her cook that Rishad would be home for dinner. He nodded briefly, used to her and Rishad's different orbits, and resigned to their indifference to the refinements of his cooking. Kirti who was ungracious, ungrateful and tyrannical, made it impossible for Devi to keep another full-time servant. No one survived Kirti's slave-driving. But long association had glued Kirti and Devi together in a bond more everlasting than cement. As far as Kirti was concerned he was still serving Ishwar. And if ever, after a quarrel over bills, she suggested he find a richer employer, he treated the suggestion with the contempt he thought it deserved. Yet since her own life had become so pared down in its demands, Kirti's talents were wasted. He only came into his own when she entertained, producing after the most summary consultation with her, dishes appropriate for the occasion. All his working life he had seen Devi in improbable situations, once even riding an elephant through flood waters to get to a cholera-ridden district across the river. Food, he was convinced, was not really her line of country. Ishwar had known more about food and about most things than she did. Kirti remembered the day long ago when he, a naive young 'mate' from the town's army mess, had been in Ishwar's employ only a few days. 'Know what this is?' It was, of course, an electric plug in the palm of Ishwar's hand, and Kirti had laughed out loud that Ishwar should think him quite that stupid. But Ishwar had gone on to explain the mystery of electricity, how the house was wired with it, and the road outside, how to mend a fuse, re-wire a lamp, the whole meaning behind putting a switch on or off. It was the first time anyone had taken trouble with him and Ishwar had later extended his education to carpentry, and after that to making and cherishing a garden.

Devi turned on the shower, and stood with her head under it, slowly coming to life again. She would have preferred to get into a dressing gown, eat something chilled and airy and catch up with the files on her study table. But Veena would mind. She brushed her hair dry. It was well-behaved and fell softly into place. The grey, noticeable now, made her face more youthful by contrast. It had become too serious a face. She had been a restless and physically active young girl and her adult work too had meant activity, travel, contacts. The missing ingredient between then and now was laughter. She and Shivraj had disgraced themselves laughing at the wrong times. They'd shared a reverence – and irreverence – for life and people. There was no one around her these days with that sense of the ridiculous, or of plain boisterous fun, least of all Rishad. She took a no longer new but delicate silvery white cotton sari out of her cupboard and put it on carefully.

'I'm sorry we've got to go out again', she told Ajaib Singh as she got into the car, 'You've had a long day.'

'Sir!' he said briskly, and started the car.

Veena, vast and beautiful, greeted her with a cry of dismay. 'But where is Rishad?'

Pinky, a voluptuous young version of Veena, came up to Devi to be kissed and congratulated, looking in her engagement finery, gold embroidered chiffon and jewels, more like a china doll than ever. Her mother introduced the neat small square young man at her elbow as 'our' future son-in-law – hers and Devi's – and Devi kissed him too.

'Why didn't Rishad come, Aunty?' asked Pinky in her childish treble, adding charitably before Devi could think of an excuse, 'I suppose he's so busy with his studies, Aunty.' Though why he should be, with Pinky doing the same course, though not of course with so much distinction, Devi couldn't say.

Two gazelle-eyed girls walked past her in flowing satin skirts that trailed the grass, and recognizing her, stopped to talk. 'Where's Rishad?' one of them wanted to know.

In his skin, having his principles for dinner, she supposed. She looked regretfully after their slender backs. Had the young always been so beautiful, or did they only nowadays have this sleek, burnished look? Why *hadn't* Rishad come? Devi felt like going to the telephone and commanding, 'Rishi, come at once. There are the most glorious looking girls here.' But he knew a lot of girls. They

36

were always ringing him up, and he went to plenty of parties, though his comments about them were niggardly. 'It was okay' could, for him mean anything from excruciating boredom to bliss. 'What did you do, drink, dance?' Yes, beer, yes, some dancing. It intrigued her because her own youth had been so protected. Young men to ride and play tennis with, and occasional hand-holding, but they'd always been in groups, never alone, and Shivraj or some older cousin had chaperoned her. 'And what did you have to eat, Rishi?' 'oh, the usual stuff. Rice, dal, veg, meat, *you* know.' Well, she didn't know. There were a dozen different ways of cooking meat and vegetables. And what had the party been *like*? Sometimes he'd provide an inestimable extra like 'Lena's mother made a casserole. She's a wonderful cook.' How did he know Lena's mother was a wonderful cook unless he'd been there before, and if he went often, then what shape, size and disposition was Lena, and why hadn't she been to their house? Or had she? Rishad was maddeningly secretive. What did he say to his friends about her, if he said anything at all? What did he actually think of her? She realized she was missing Rishad terribly.

The party was out in the garden, night flower scents surrounding them, the electrically-lit red and blue brilliance of hundreds of bulbs outdoing the softer illumination of oil lamps along the driveway. Lights streamed from every window of the house. Like everything at Veena and Vijay's, it was almost too much to take in, an opulence of which one soon lost track and simply drowned in. Today was a special day, but every day was a little like that here. Devi enviously counted the number of juices being served along with stronger drinks. Fresh tomato, fresh mulberry, fresh mango, fresh tamarind. Two she couldn't identify.

'You can leave three of those here for me to taste,' she told the bearer who grinned and set them down on a table near her.

Pistachio, almond and coconut 'barfis' of melting sweetness were being passed, their silver 'varakh' still glistening and puffy over them. And spicy kebabs that dissolved like cream in your mouth. A bearer came to her with a message from Vijay's father.

She crossed the lawn to where he was presiding, smooth-skinned and sardonic in his middle seventies, over a gathering of his own selection. He gave her an appreciative look, said, 'What is that fool government of yours going to do next?' and invited her to sit beside him. The old gentleman, who found his son, his daughter-in-law and his grandchildren exceedingly boring, liked nothing better than a sparring match with Devi. He had made money in his time when money had not had such an appallingly vulgar life of its own, divorced from the life around it. He was bored stiff with money, too, and the people it bred.

'How is the champion of the poor?' he enquired.

'The Prime Minister is very well,' Devi replied formally.

'I have it on good authority that you spoke against me at a party last night,' he mimicked the querulous tones of the country's leader, 'Anybody that touchy can't be very well.'

'Don't be dreadful, Papaji, it's your granddaughter's engagement party'

He said in a lower tone, 'Yes and don't they look like the cat that swallowed the canary now they've betrothed her to three banks and a brewery. Vijay isn't sending her back to university now. Yesterday's trouble gives him an excuse not to.'

'Oh, that's a pity, when she's already in her final year.'

'I hear your friend Usman Ali won't have the police on campus. Is that wise?'

A prickle of anxiety needled Devi. She had tried to leave it behind at home, at least for this evening. She said, 'I suppose he knows best.'

He watched her shrewdly, 'You'd better advise him to have the police. These aren't Shivraj's times.'

'Shivraj's times? Papaji, you talk as if Shivraj's times were decades ago.' She told herself, but this *is* another time, why do I lie?

'They were. This bunch put everything he stood for on his funeral pyre with him. First casualty, common sense. Revolution my left toe. Revolution in a cream puff with the cream all going to them. Plenty from this one house, let me tell you.'

He did not have to tell her. Vijay was one of the big new donors to the Party.

'There's quite a lot of cream left around here,' she remarked.

'Between here and your bunch is where it is.' He lifted his chin toward the flurry of arrival as the Minister for Minerals and Metals alighted from his car. 'That one's women are costing more and more.'

'How abstemious were you at his age?'

'I wasn't. But Party funds didn't pay my fornication bills.'

Veena saw Devi and taking no notice of her father-in-law's protests took her away. 'I've been looking everywhere for you. I should have known Papaji had cornered you. Come inside and see Pinky's trousseau. I didn't want to return anything till you'd seen what we'd chosen.'

Devi picked up one of the juice glasses, tempting, purple, ice-cold, and followed Veena in. The trousseau, along with all the saris that would now be returned to the shops, filled one of the bedrooms. Devi saw pyramids, mounds, layers of saris, folded neatly on the beds, hung like rainbows over a sofa, pleated and fanned out across the backs of chairs to show off their colours. In a corner of the room a senior aunt sat on the carpet talking earnestly to the family jeweller who had called with designs and precious stones for her selection. His assistant sat cross-legged in another part of the room, an unshaded electric lamp on the floor near him, washing loose pearls in a china bowl with Pinky's ayah diligently looking on. He dried them carefully and arranged them in the shape of a necklace on a square of black cloth, getting ready to thread and knot each one on a strong silk cord.

'Why is he doing this at night?'

'There's so much to get done, and Pinky needs her pearls.'

Veena picked up an almond 'barfi' from a dish near her, broke it in two, popped one half into Devi's mouth, the other into her own. She sent the ayah to call Pinky and the girl came in to have some of her trousseau saris held up against her face to see how they suited her in this light.

'It's a stunning collection,' said Devi.

'Do you approve? Then shall we send the others back now?' asked Veena.

Devi turned to Pinky. 'What does the bride-to-be think? Are you pleased with your trousseau, Pinky?'

'Oh yes, Aunty.'

'Have you been seeing a lot of Arvind?'

'No Aunty. He's posted in Bombay. He's only come for the engagement. He's going back tomorrow.'

'You must tell me what you want for a wedding present.'

Pinky's brow reflected the enormous effort of thinking. 'You decide, Aunty. You'll know best.'

Devi, who had known Pinky since she was born, six weeks after Rishad, had never known her other than plump, sweet and obedient. The most awful disaster – a slap from teacher at school, a cancelled treat when she got fever, a tooth extraction – did no more than ruffle that doll face. She *was* rather a pudding, but a good little pudding, and everyone couldn't be geniuses plotting to overthrow things, if that was what geniuses did. Veena led the way to the drawing room.

'Let's sit here for a bit,' she said, 'I never see you for a chat since you became a Minister.'

And that was only a few months ago. They talked as if decades had elapsed. Perhaps they had, between an understood world and the chemically different present. In Veena's drawing room the orange, red and bronze of the room's winter furnishings had been replaced by cool colours when the warm weather began. Masses of crystal from Veena and Vijay's recent trip to Europe stood on glass shelves, too dense a dazzle of it. Illuminated shelved recesses paraded bronze antique images. Woodwork was radiantly glossy. Carpets of different sizes but each a costly showpiece of iridescent colour and design joined to cover the floor. It had all been there before, but not in such profusion. Hard to put one's finger on the moment and style of change. In contrast with the rest of the room a painting, its opal moonlit tones, somehow virginal in this light, hung above the marble fireplace chastely framed in narrow natural wood. Devi had helped Veena choose it at an exhibition and had persuaded her not to buy an ornate frame for it. Her eyes rested on it, a refuge from the room's opulence.

Veena helped herself to a kebab from a bearer passing through the room.

'I'm exhausted,' she said, 'Have I lost any weight?'

'No, of course not. You've been eating all evening.'

'I wasn't meant to be thin.'

'You were meant to be exactly as you are, so stop bothering about being thin.'

Veena looked perfect as usual, a coiffure like black lacquer, never a grey hair visible, her complexion flawless, her hands and nails straight from the manicurist, her sari a fabulous pale pink embroidered cotton, new, and an original like the rest, an air of lotions and ointments and lingering in perfumed baths about her. Even her fat had perfection. She was ripe, round and firm.

'But I want to be like *you*' moaned Veena with comic insistence, 'I've always wanted to be like you. Devi, you must tint your hair. A touch of grey was all right, but there's more now.'

'It would take too much time and fuss,' objected Devi, 'I never even used a contraceptive all through my marriage. I never could manage anything mechanical. Pills must be a godsend.'

'They are. But you don't have to manage anything. Just go to my hairdresser.'

'I couldn't. Too much fuss. The very idea of contraceptives used to make me feel something was stuck in my throat.'

'Choking,' Veena explained patiently, 'is connected with the windpipe. Contraceptives – '

'I know. It's just one of my stupidities.'

'Well you were lucky. If I'd left contraception to Vijay, I'd have had ten children instead of four. After his fifth double whisky Vijay wouldn't know a contraceptive from a cow bell.'

'Veena, how much does Pinky know about sex?'

'There you go being modern. What do you want her to know? Her in-laws are very conservative. They don't want one of these smart newfangled girls.'

'Still – "began Devi doubtfully.

'You and I did all right,' interrupted Veena, 'It's rubbish, this modern business about knowing everything before you marry.' Parents had chosen one's husband, but then, as sometimes happened, as had happened to Devi, one fell tenderly, distractedly in love with him. But the Pinky-Arvind combine didn't strike her that way. Veena said with a ring of triumph in her voice, 'Pinky couldn't have done better, Devi. How do you like the boy?'

'Did she choose him herself?'

'Yes, of course. As soon as we heard about him we arranged a meeting. And then we asked Pinky how she liked him. We put it to her frankly like that. And she gave her consent.'

'I hope it's going to be all right.'

We're a society at the crossroads, all right, as the professors in the Cabinet keep saying, thought Devi. But they don't realize how many different crossroads we're at, some in yesterday, some in tomorrow, some in the Middle Ages. Rishad was already half in tomorrow. The gazelle-eyed girls at this party – God knew what went on in their minds – but they looked like today's blossoms. Girls like Pinky lived as their mothers and grandmothers had. And somewhere in this confusion of change was Madhu, so savagely used, and her tormentors. To bring all these cross-roads together needed an artist. It was a task of the imagination. Her friends thought she missed Shivraj. She did. But his death had involved the whole country. Her grief had been shared, diminished. And she felt even closer to him since he had died. She had not hated him for dying, hadn't missed him searingly, a black vacuum where feeling had been, as she had missed Ishwar after his death. What she missed was the sense of values Shivraj had planted like roses with his two hands. It was their fragrance, something as ephemeral as that, that had bound the country together in a unity, not any hidebound principle or rule from a book.

'Where is my girl friend?' roared a voice from the verandah, and Veena's husband came in, pulling Devi up from the sofa, putting a heavy arm about her shoulders, 'Why are you hiding the light of my life in this room?' he accused his wife.

'The light of your life has been looking at your daughter's trousseau,' said Veena placidly, 'and giving me good advice.'

'We all need her advice,' Vijay rumbled near Devi's ear, 'She's the only Minister who understands me.' He gave Devi's shoulders a squeeze, then looked disbelievingly at the drink in her hand. 'What is this?' he roared. A bearer was summoned to bring whisky (Scotch, he bellowed.) and soda (separately). He looked at Devi, hurt. 'And at my eldest daughter's engagement, too.'

'You know I don't like the taste of whisky,' Devi said.

Vijay remembered. I've got some champagne on ice. What am I keeping it for? Veena's relations and mine are eating us out of house and home and they're not going to get champagne on top of it.'

Vijay said it goodnaturedly. She knew he adored his enormous thriving family and was in his element surrounded by it. The eldest son of a family who had lost their home and assets at Partition, Vijay and his brothers had set up business all over again in Delhi. There had not been much time in that struggle against adversity to cultivate the graces of living, only its emblems. Vijay's friends had to take him and his roar in their stride. Devi watched with a pang as her delicious, priceless, fresh juice was taken away and a distinguished wine glass of Czech crystal produced for champagne.

'Stop wrinkling your nose. Everybody else has a caterer's glass. This is special for you. And you can't toast my daughter in one of Veena's endless juices.'

The champagne was presented, frosty from the refrigerator, opened and poured by Vijay. It brought Devi an unaccustomed pleasant intoxication. So, in a way, did this house with its perpetual excited bustle, a family bustle, with relations come together from all over the country for the wedding. But it was not only the wedding. Family always spilled over in a warm delightful confusion in Veena's house. Her own trimmer, almost relation-less set up seemed gaunt in contrast. A frighteningly small unit, two people, herself and Rishad, going different ways. No surrounding friendliness for either of them to take comfort in. A big family sometimes performed that function, cushioned you against shocks, put ups and downs into focus, was simply there, a broad soft bosom. Vijay re-filled her champagne glass. Other guests had come into the room. She could hear Vijay urging everyone to drink, bearers everywhere filling glasses, the triumvirate of whisky, soda, water, borne in and out of the crowd like a lever accelerating the heat and noise and rhythm of the party until they reached a steady controlled pitch and pressure and drummed there. Her anxiety kept mounting to the surface and knocking against it. Usman's injuries and all that had led to them. The Ministry. Rishad. The whole puzzling present. One of Pinky's sisters had put music on the stereo and in the verandah alongside young people were dancing. The clock above the mantelpiece tinkled courteously. Its nine thin tuneful chimes could scarcely be heard, a discordant silvery stripe across the plateau of solid sound. Devi went into Veena's bedroom, sat down on Veena's side of the bed and dialled Usman's number.

'Did I disturb you at dinner? I wanted to ring earlier but I got waylaid by champagne. Have you been to the doctor today? What did he say?' The words hurried out almost before she knew who had picked up the receiver. But it was Usman.

'We've had dinner.' There was a pause. He might have been closing a door, then he asked, 'Where are you?'

'I thought I'd told you. At the Puris'.'

'You did not. And you know I like to know these things. Where is the Puris' telephone?'

'In their bedroom. Are you really all right?'

'Yes. Do they have a double bed?.'

Devi looked behind her.

'Treble by the look of it. It's vast. And fluffy. Lots of frills and pillows.'

'Where do they get sheets that size?'

'Usman,' she could hear the strain in her own voice, 'I want to know exactly how you are.'

He told her.

'Shahbano,' he added quietly, 'at this minute I feel remarkably well. Can't you tell by my voice?'

Devi was normally so un-anxious, so well-balanced in her certainties, he had never before needed to re-inforce her confidence. Everything in him yearned to do so now, to reach out to her in affection and strength. And because her brother's death had created a new bond between them, one of work.

Devi smiled into the telephone, 'Yes, I can tell.'

They spoke on the telephone more often than they met, usually on official matters, but telephoning had become an outlet too for Usman's gifted and versatile sensuality. Today, insensitive to everything but reassurance, she felt only relief at the sound of his voice and the gratitude that any contact with him brought her. She had much to be grateful to him for, perhaps the wholeness and health of her being.

'What does champagne taste like?' he asked.

'I keep forgetting you don't drink. I like it. You should try it.'

'Introduce me to the Puris then. I'm going to try a lot of things once I'm out from behind the barricade.'

A woman came into the room, examined her mouth at Veena's

44

mirror and went into the bathroom. Devi said goodnight to Usman and put the phone down.

It was nearly midnight when she got home to find her mail still lying on the hall table. She took it to her bedroom, undressed, and got into bed to read it. She had not recognized the letter from England because Michael Calvert had never written to her before. She read it slowly three times. A good letter, beautifully expressive, about Shivraj. She had had one from Michael after Shivraj's death and it had been full and expressive too. The personal part of the letter was a request. He would be arriving in Delhi in early September to finish work on his book. Would she find him a flat or a small house? With much love, Michael. A p.s. below said he had not intended to trouble her, knowing how busy she must be, but now that he had, would she help? He'd be so grateful for a line in reply. Love again, Michael.

5

Michael Calvert had been born in India in a family that had, on both sides, been connected with India. He had been sent home to school at the age of eight, not to return again until the war, when he found himself defending His Majesty's empire overseas. In his eagerness to re-discover the haunts of his childhood he went from Calcutta to Kashmir on leave, travelling sixteen hundred miles, through the immensity and variety of the country he was seeing as an adult for the first time. Pahalgam in the Kashmir Valley, at an altitude of seven thousand feet, exhilarated him with its dark pine forests and rushing streams. On his second day there he heard there was to be a public meeting. He came across it out in the open, a man in white talking to what looked like a sea of people on the undulating hill terrain. He was reminded of the Sermon on the Mount, only that must have been a smaller gathering in a narrower land. He did not understand a word that was said but he could not tear himself away. The scene was knit together in a harmony of its own, man, hillside and listeners inseparably interwoven. Michael sensed he was watching a great event. The war he had come to fight had not rippled the surface of life here on this hill, and this timeless scene expressed an urge older, profounder than war. He felt that this man and his listeners held the key to the future, and the future began a day later when the Valley echoed with the news of Shivraj's arrest and removal to prison until the war's end.

Michael returned to India when the war was over to write for a British newspaper. The two years before independence were the most eventful of his own life. He reported on political developments and rang the curtain down over empire before those at Whitehall did. He wrote of a new era, symbolized for him by the man on the hillside, at a time when British missions to discuss the terms of the transfer of power were failing, and solutions were being discarded one after another. None of that mattered to Michael. The world had changed and independence was a matter of months or weeks. A new dawn was breaking in Britain, too, with the coming of a government that recognized the fact. Later his editor remarked, 'You're the only person I've ever known, Michael, who has called Attlee a revolutionary. I'm not sure I should allow that to pass.' Wasn't he? Michael had demanded. What else was a man who ended empire? Michael's writing had the freshness of youth and conviction and his attachment to India had no spiritual craving or content. The chief attraction for him was a mentality that knew how to leave people alone. There had been no fierce either-or mentality here, no murder of one idea or loyalty to make room for another. They all seemed to do well enough in their separate ways, and Shivraj seemed to symbolize that too. Walking along Rajpath in Delhi, its peaceful lawns scattered with evening walkers and balloon and bangle sellers, he thought of the use made of other commanding avenues he had seen during the war. This one at least would never resound to goosestepping boots or mass mania of any kind. One day, trying to cross a road through a jostling crowd, he had seen in a mirror hanging outside a panwalla's shop, a man much bigger and taller than those around him, blond, strange and red in the face, yet wearing the pyjama-kurta of the crowd. It startled him to realize it was himself. At some time during those two years he had started to wear Indian clothes. They were cooler. He had changed in other ways. He must have talked more, gestured more, and come to know more people then than ever afterward. At the end of that period he was a minor celebrity, though even earlier his sympathies for Indian aspiration had become well known. He was, however, at the start of this whole experience, still wearing a suit and superfluities like shoes and socks and ties, when he met Shivraj, face to face this time, once again in Kashmir, soon after his release. With Shivraj was his sister, in the gathering on the sloping lawns of the guest house where they were staying, the sunlit enchantment of the Valley spread like a festival around them.

He had observed her with interest as she watched her brother not five yards away, her face showing pride and concern as he talked to the journalists who had assembled to welcome his release from his final imprisonment. Michael, one of the journalists, stayed beside her, sensing a relationship that might fill a big gap in his knowledge

47

of Shivraj. They did not look particularly alike. The man's face, older, bore the marks of long isolation, prison diet and the dead hand of prison routine. An austere face, all planes and angles, deeply preoccupied and shadowed. Hers, softly contoured, had the glow of health, her eyes the velvety sheen and triangular look of the pansies she was holding. He matched the rightness of the posies and garlands people had brought for Shivraj, piled on the tea table near her. The two of them were yet somehow similar and when they had looked at each other, Michael had known that other deeper resemblances bound them. He wanted to say impetuously, 'You love him dearly.' It would be a natural affirmation, like the light on the lake, while political programmes, at this moment of release and rejoicing, seemed far distant. She recognized his name as soon as he introduced himself and said warmly, 'We have a lot to thank you for, Mr. Calvert.'

The 'we' was quite natural. She and her brother, she meant, or she might have been speaking for her countrymen in general. Yet it had an imperial touch, though he could not say why he thought so. She had moved freely among the guests, talking with a gaiety and vitality they found irresistible. He remembered being told once that people were always falling in love with her. He realized he was staring at her. Devi invited him to sit down – an excellent opportunity to ask her some important questions about Shivraj's plans – and he could think of nothing except the look of pansies her eyes had, a dark-bright, brown-purple look, a look utterly impossible to mix up with political negotiations. It was absurd how he had sat there not saying a word, like the idiot in the class, while she, taking his interest for granted, had given him a full and fluent account in precise language of what she thought were the possibilities ahead. Michael wondered later if there had been some calculation in his staying with her, apart from her eyes. Had he known she would suggest after the others left, that he should stay on to dinner with them, opening the way to informality with Shivraj? Though that would not explain what happened incomprehensibly a few days after Shivraj left. He knew, when Devi took over his life, that important events are pre-destined. Would any man in his right mind, with the use of his will and judgement, have chosen to go headlong into that madness? His own conduct, even when he thought about it all these years later, astonished him, There he'd been, lost to the world on hillsides and near streams, with no idea or hope of permanence, nor the opposite casual comfort of a decorous, soon to be forgotten affair. This had been a new principality of need and desire, nothing to do with what he had known of himself till then, and the years had done little to free him of her bewildering charm. As if it had not been enough to be with her in that extraordinary situation, he had been agonized about being a successful lover, somehow capturing and holding her, at least in imagination, forever.

Sleeping with Devi was a quaint misnomer for the most acutely awake time of his life. They had not slept the first or any other time. No two had ever been further from sleep. Michael remembered to begin with the sheer physical strain surrounding their love-making. They had had to get miles away from Srinagar to avoid the risk of being seen, to all sorts of unlikely places. He recalled, as if it were yesterday, his terrible alertness to every sound and sight, real or fancied. The temple they had come to one afternoon was off the motor road, a thirteen hundred-year-old glory. Remote, but tourists came all the time. It was one of the sights to see. Lunch uneaten they lay against an inner wall, just out of the sun, near them a fragment of broken Grecian-looking colonnade they had fondly hoped would screen them from the road. But someone would appear for sure, Michael was convinced. The village was only a mile away. Or a goatherd might come with his silly animals round that projecting rock, or horror of horrors, a bunch of half-hostile village women, incredulous and derisive at their find. Of all this Devi, moaning and murmuring exquisitely and unintelligibly beneath him, was quite oblivious. He looked quickly away from her face, seized on the goatherd, the women, anything that would divert him from her eyes. The sun-baked road, the hill behind it, a goatherd on that, long-robed, skull-capped, grazing his flock. Michael repeated verses from the Bible, running them into each other punctuation-less, until he put a hand over her mouth to muffle her cry, and in infinite gratitude collapsed beside her. Drawn upward into the empty uninterrupted blue, all concentration blessedly ebbing from him, he fancied lovers in this rice-growing valley would say 'Thy belly is like an heap of rice', not wheat, and when they said 'Thou art fair, my love,' they would mean young willows, lotus honey and saffron. He

49

would lie looking at the sublime blue overhead partly to delay the supreme pleasure of turning his head and looking at last at her face. It had been that way until she had said softly one day as he lay beside her, 'Darling Michael, I'm sorry you have to work so hard. Is love-making always so hard on men?' And he had told her he wasn't men. He was caught up in an unbearable enchantment with a creature of the woods who had pine needles in her hair and the breath of pines on her skin, 'But darling Michael', she had laughed, 'you're not to work so hard. I'm not even very – *ept* – is that a word? Whatever I might have known, I've forgotten,' She did not otherwise mention her widowhood. But a woman like her must have had lovers. Hadn't she? 'Good heavens. When would I have had them, and where? If I'd had a lover the whole country would have known about it.' Which didn't quite seem to answer the question.

He had work to do, a piece to write on Shivraj, and his was the fullest to appear in the press, a portrait richer for Devi's re-collections. He did not put these down but they became the background of his understanding of Shivraj, of what he'd been like before fame and destiny took him over, the early little-known mosaic. He and Devi sat and talked on the terrace of the houseboat she had taken on the Nagin lake when Shivraj left for Delhi, drinking Kashmiri tea cooked in a samovar in front of them with sugar, cinnamon and green almonds, while Rishad played in long grass on the bank in the giant shade of three cathedral-like chinars. The Nagin changed colour and mood, glassy gold with a dusty glitter under the afternoon sun, soft steel at twilight, crumpled under rain, and became woven with Devi's talk about Shivraj. The biography of Shivraj might well deliver itself up whole from the waters and jewel colours of the Nagin, he thought years later, their awareness of the lake had so saturated all they said.

'He'd been back I think three or four years from university, and we'd been out riding,' said Devi, 'It was late evening and we were on our way home along a road that took us past a stretch of fields. Normally that's a great bloomy expanse of wheat at that time of year, but it was all burnt-out with drought. We saw a huge blur moving across it in the distance and it turned out to be a procession of "kisans", their "lathis" across their shoulders, coming back from a council they'd called in a neighbouring village. I'll never forget their cry as it reached us across the fields – "Sita Ram" – drawn out like streamers in the wind, half sung, half called. It was so antique and so thrilling the way it seemed to rise up out of the soil. We got off our horses and walked them over to the procession and started talking to the "kisans". Soon we were all sitting in a circle talking about the council they had attended, about the effects of the drought and what help they were getting for it. When we were going home, Shivraj said, "I dont like the word 'masses'. It lumps humanness into a *thing*, like a mass of clay, for someone *else's* use." We wondered what word would be better and decided on "multitude". One person multiplied by many, but at least human persons. It's like suffering.'

'What is?' asked Michael, finding it hard to keep up with her.

'Shivraj said once that suffering may be common, but it's not a common bond. It's an individual hell. A person in agony doesn't think of anyone but himself. He can't. He's wrapped around with his own pain.' She poured fresh tea into both their cups. 'There's no more suffering in the world than one person can endure.'

'Who said that, you or Shivraj?'

'What does it matter, Michael? It's the same thing. We were twins, born six years apart.'

Michael imagined Devi, one with her horse in her control and delight in it, and fell in love all over again with the girl she had been.

'I saw you thinking that day at the party how worn he looked,' said Devi, 'what prison had done to him. But it didn't, you know. He went to prison the way a monk goes to a monastery. He was even happy, writing, thinking, growing. It was I who dragged him around, made him ride with me and take the boat out on the river. Maybe he was the inside and I was the outside of the same person.'

Michael saw a girl in flower, radiant in her youth and health, on horseback again, her hair flying back in the wind, her companion close behind her; a girl and her companion in a boat, at the wrong time of day when the river drove boats ashore, a ribbed and bony river folded in lengthening shadow between silent sands. And then, a picture as distinct, of a family enlarged by friends and relations at a long polished table reflecting light from the candelabra above it, the boy and girl, cherished as roses, facing each other across it. Leaving it later to walk arm in arm in the light of the stars. The Pharaohs had married their sisters.

He said abruptly, 'Devi, what are we going to do after we get to Delhi?'

'Do?'

'About each other. How are we going to meet?' He added irritated, 'it would be a change to get to a proper bed.'

He needed some immediate assurance of a future with her.

'It's going to be a problem,' she said.

The problem of when and where to make love to Devi loomed up in Delhi, putting him into a fury, so that they spent most of their time quarrelling. Hotel-building had not yet begun on any scale and the one or two there were were about as private as Chandni Chowk. In Delhi everybody knew everybody, and Devi was public property, sharing Shivraj's house, and perpetually in the limelight. Their meetings were tense. She seemed all given to her brother, his life, his needs. She had no other life. Michael had confronted her passionately with the ruins of their summer, and when she would not discuss it, delivered an ultimatum. She must marry him. Devi had looked shocked and strained.

'I can't do the things other people do.'

In an ugly scene, one of the last, he had shouted at her, 'What are you, the ghost of your brother?'

'If that's what I am it's enough for me.' She had said it in a stricken way but he knew there was no changing her mind.

This bloody country, he had raged, this bloody bloody country. Nothing and no one is good enough for it. May it sicken and rot of its own arrogance. And he had consigned it, and her, to damnation and left. He smarted under the irony, too, of departing, unwept, like the rest of the British. The flight to England had drained him of his anger and humiliation. In a very real sense he felt he had left home.

Michael had progressed a long way into his writing. In the months after Shivraj's death he had reconstructed the Shivraj years as he had known and studied them. He had had to decide what kind of book it was going to be, Shivraj against the panorama of his times or a more individual portrait, and he had chosen the latter.

The choice had yielded up insights he had forgotten he possessed about Shivraj. He had begun to write with ease, images of the past, conversations, a look, an emphasis coming back to him with an illumined clarity. Shivraj had been a political animal, but a man with interests, too, from the earth's crust to astronomy; with friends, not only followers. It would have been a pity to confine him to a political platform, hung with an ideology. Michael found he was probing a complicated personal development only partly related to a particular man and his century. The creative lifetime has a universal voice and colour. Shivraj's early writing had an appealing confessional quality: 'I am becoming more and more uncomfortable in the life I am living. I am nearly twenty-one and I know nothing really real of the society I live in. How much longer can I go on like this?' Innumerable young men had ached for the 'really real'. There was much in common, too, between all struggles for liberation, the commonest factor, uncertainty. Reading page after page of the documents still in the British Government's possession, Michael had experienced it keenly. 'I'm not sure where I'll be this time next week.' 'I wonder when we shall meet again.' 'I don't yet know what our next move ought to be.' An enormous psychological question mark stamped on official and private deliberations in letters to friends and colleagues. What would tomorrow bring? In the West during the atomic end-of-the-world fear this had thrown up a decade or more of deep gloom in philosophy and literature and a sense of personal injury and anger. Here in these letters uncertainty was a travelling companion.

And now that Shivraj was dead Michael began to see him as part of a race — descendant of the great migration that journeyed through the Indus Valley into the plain. Strangers in a strange land who came and fell in love and remained to build on the banks of the Ganges a giant civilization of enormous complexity. That thread of almost mystical attachment to the land, its rivers and hills, ran through many of Shivraj's writings, even the most mundane of his speeches, another quality shared with many liberators of their people from foreign domination.

Michael looked up from his writing and out of his window, seeing not the blur of fog on the playing field below him, and passers-by in unexpected woollens again, but a hundred yards of immaculate lawn blocked by bougainvillea the colour of baked brick at its far end. Beyond it would be the grove of evergreens so unusual in a Delhi garden, and to the right the kumquat trees whose miniature sour oranges Devi had had preserved in syrup for Shivraj's table. How often he had walked up and down that lawn with Shivraj, asking questions. The light and grass were a vivid green-gold under the sun. They blended luminously into a landscape where he could see a younger Devi come out of the house with the quick eager walk so characteristic of her, and join her brother on the lawn, taking his arm, flicking a speck off the sleeve of his kurta. The physical contact between them was so constant, hands touching, his head bent to hers. Michael could see the exact shape of her finders on Shivraj's arm, and two small bright birds on a bush near them open their wings and fly away. In that house, in the room upstairs, Shivraj's close colleagues and that outer circle that had so ingeniously ousted them, with ringing promises of a quick transformation unlettered people will believe, must have gathered in whispered conclave even before his body was cold. Michael had spent as much time during the last ten years in the company of the dead as of the living. He had made enough studies of leadership to know that a leader's death plus-one-minute created new circumstances in all but the stablest societies. That this had happened in India was not surprising. But it left him wondering. Upstairs, too, Devi had once taken the enormous risk of admitting him to her room when in a stormy quarrel he had demanded a few minutes alone with her. The quarrel had been left outside the room. Devi unlike most women had had a complete absorption with love-making, everything forgotten while her welling need consumed her and while she yielded to his. He had never before or after been so abject. Lying by her side, he had pleaded, 'Darling, don't you see we can't go on like this? What's wrong with me? Why won't I do?'

She had replied, 'It has nothing to do with you, Michael, but being English, that's what you can't understand.'

'Then explain, for God's sake.'

'I have a duty to Shivraj.'

Really, it was monstrous. Duty he understood, to a husband or wife or child. What duty was this? She tried to explain.

'It is a big word – for us. It is not something chilly and punishing.

54

It's almost religion. Without it, my life would have no meaning.'

Without him, then, it would, he had retorted bitterly.

'I wouldn't be able to live with myself,' she said patiently.

With herself, with Shivraj, it was all the same thing, they were so much flesh of each other's flesh, their very souls mixed. He had been jealous of Shivraj. He should have hated him, but he had grown to love him instead, so he, too, had got entangled in the strange contradiction. He had understood Devi after all, wretched and unwilling though he had been, he had understood.

It was his last evening in London and he was taking Nell out to dinner. Somewhere nice, she had said, so that she could wear a new black dress. Nell had not seen and done everything. There were pleasures he could still uncover for her. He took her to a small French restaurant he had discovered. The few times he had eaten there he had been reminded what food was, and what insipid and disgraceful substitutes passed as food in between. Nothing bohemian here, the atmosphere was disciplined and mellowed with the quality of its offerings. The room was severe with its immaculate white walls, its soundless reverent service and its knowledgeable clientele. Three unframed abstracts, their paint laid on thick and lustrous with the palette knife, provided rectangles of arresting colour along one wall. They ate wonderful trout, peas, fresh young greens only the French knew when to pick and how to serve, soft ripe cheese, and drank a fragrant wine.

'What an atmosphere,' said Nell, 'it might be a temple, with everyone worshipping the food.'

There was talk but it was subdued, a secondary consideration to eating, and laughter was low and satisfied. Nell herself was eating with obvious zest.

'Temples, at least the ones I've seen in India, are noisy and usually dirty places.' Michael told her, 'In fact it's a noisy country.'

'Is it? I imagined it peaceful.'

He described a residential neighbourhood he had lived in in Delhi where he had been woken shatteringly on the dot of four each morning by religious services performed over a microphone. After a while, he told her, all the noise and heat and colour got stamped into your brain, an indelible violent photograph that was impossible to wipe out, and everything else was insipid and correct in comparison. He thought suddenly of Lydia. Nell looking shrewdly at him, said that that was why since coming home he had played with everything not connected with his writing. It was this 'violent indelible past' of his.

'Why did you put up with me at all?' he asked her, always regretful about any harm he may have done her.

'I didn't put up with you. I was in love. You were a big experience. And I'm glad it's over. So don't feel guilty about me. Can I have more cheese?'

Nell slipped her arm through his as he walked her back to her flat through the cold crisp early autumn dark, describing the new furniture she was exhibiting next month and, second in priority, a man she'd met. Michael, infected by her youth and high spirits, smiled as he listened. When the door closed behind her, he stood for a minute, grateful for the naturalness of this ending. The last few days had had an unreality for him, the September sun coming and going hesitantly on a scene of which he was no part any more. He knew that whatever happened to him in India, he would return to a very difficult life.

Rishad guessed from its position at the side of the house and the bathroom near it, that it was a bedroom, though all he could see of the room's interior from the street was a segment of mirror, kindled by flashes of sun. It was too high up on the wall to reflect anything in the room, a face or a passing figure. A mirror with nothing reflected in it. Little ironies like this cropped up every now and then to underscore his resolve. Not that his resolve needed bolstering. But these cropped up like signposts pointing out this was the way and no mistake. Here, for example, was a useless mirror – but it reflected something all right – the whole rotten system propping the means to buy useless mirrors. For six days now Rishad's calculations had centred on the narrow strip of glass he could see even from where he stood, winking in the sun.

They had sectioned the neighbourhood among the four of them, and this street, in old Delhi, had been assigned to him. It wasn't the problem of entry that had made him wait across the street from the house for several days. He was acquainting himself with the habits of its occupants. A small, thin balding man, a scarecrow of a girl, and a grizzled old servant with the look of a tough root-vegetable about him were the ones he had seen. Entry was no problem. The better-off-class branded alien by him though he belonged to it – left everything wide open, a mark of its casual overlordship in a country, a city, where no one had ever challenged the hoary status quo. Rishad waited because he was a perfectionist. He took pride in a job well done and this job had to be meticulously done at a time of day when no one was about.

In this as in so many other parts of the new and old city, trees lined both sides of the street. But on oppressive windless days like this there was no shade even under a tree. Not a leaf rustled. He looked up at the sky. It was like curdled milk and an unbearably shiny glare glanced off it. He felt if he could just reach up with a stick and stir it, it would rain. *Now*, he told himself. He crossed the street, stopping once behind a hibiscus bush near the gate to make sure again, and walked in through a side door into the bedroom, his target. The choice was deliberate. Ransack a drawing room and though it created a commotion it did not sow terror. He and the others had been at it weeks now and they knew. A bedroom was something else again. Expertly ripped and savaged it revealed practised, ruthless intent. It panicked a household, a street, a neighbourhood. Panic was an artist's creation, the fifth person, his group called it. Where was the fifth person today, they would ask each other, not in banter, in dead earnest. The answer guided their assessment at the end of the day of where they should strike next.

Panic was like a gas. You could release it according to plan, in jets and spurts or in long slow expulsion, depending on what you intended. Enough of it could reduce a household or a neighbourhood to jelly. And at the right moment, with enough of it spread around, came the star stroke. Rishad had not killed, though the first injunction was: if anyone saw you or tried to stop you, kill. Once they planned a killing, however, they used a squad of twelve or thirteen-year-olds to do it, and trained them to do it scientifically. If possible they supervised the finale themselves: ambush in a one-way street, the knife too swift to permit a cry, almost no blood. The technique helped to widen the gap between murder and discovery. *No stealing* had to be drummed into the little boys. No taking a single thing off the body. If they did and were caught they were severely punished and threatened with expulsion. This cult of violence had to be clean, cold and disciplined, unaided by motive, by drugs or mental aberration. This was the violence of the sane with a passion for justice. To build a new world the old one had to be razed to the ground. The way to do it was through the systematic creation of panic. Panic to chaos to ruin. And out of ruin open revolt and power. Only then could the new social order arise. Not Utopia. Just food in the stomach and a decent wage. Utopia for the poor and the downtrodden. An Indian Utopia.

Indoors the room looked shabby. Even the mirror, with the conceit of a garland of gilt fruit carved into its frame, looked old and spotted, its frame cracked and faded. The cotton bedspreads were faded too. He dragged them off the beds to the floor, then the rest of the bed linen. He felt justified when he saw two hundred and fifty rupees worth each of fat spongy foam rubber mattress covered in printed cotton opulently open to his knife. He dealt with both. He defaced the walls. He collected the glass bottles on the dressing table and smashed them carefully with a brick he had left in the verandah just outside. He broke what he could of the plywood drawers. There was a wrist watch and some five rupee notes in one of them. He laid these neatly on top of the dressing table.

He came to the mirror. A few blows of his knife handle splintered the frame easily. The tough mirror surface took longer, finally surrendering in subdued crashes. A triangle of it fell soundless to the carpet as he stepped aside. He was breaking the legs of a bedside table when he saw her out of the corner of his eye. He swung round to confront the girl. She looked drained and paralysed, insubstantial as a ghost. She must be the daughter, the scarecrow he had seen come and go with books under her arm. He advanced on her as he knew he must.

'Wait!' she gasped, 'I'll help you!'

And that stopped him. The second injunction was: find helpers, recruit followers. More and more groups of four had grown out of the original cell at the university. She came into the room.

'The cupboard.' He had to lip-read her words.

He pulled open the door. Between them they hauled saris off hangers, tidy piles of clothes off shelves. She fetched scissors from the dressing table. He used his knife. Twenty minutes later when they stood over the shambles, the girl's face gave Rishad a shock. She was transformed, her cheeks flushed. Even the thin hands at the end of her fragile breakable-looking wrists were animated. He put his knife away.

'I'm off,' he said.

'Wait!'

'Well?'

'I – please see me again.'

The question was how not to. Her sudden appearance on the scene had unnerved him. He was not sure what the consequences of it would be. But she had helped. She might even be of use. Why not a girl recruit as well? He told her he was going to the campus coffee shop and would be there for an hour. He walked without haste to the street corner near the bus stand where he had left his motor cycle, and unlocked it. He was trembling. Suppose she had raised an alarm or if he had had to silence her before she could? Everything around Rishad, the shrill sunlight, even the sky, sweated, pressing down on him. But there was no sign of rain. The rain's refusal held the city in a suffocating stranglehold, allowing it neither to come to life nor die. Even the weather these days under-scored his resolve, a constant reminder that this in-between state, neither life nor death, was what many people lived in. His shirt clung to his chest and back, but some of his fear left him as he started his motor cycle and rode out of the empty street toward the ordinary world, his world.

In the coffee shop, with its odours of fresh hot coffee and frying food and the marks left by seventy years of student clientele on tables, chairs and even the floor, he felt calmer. He waved to a group he recognized and sat down at a table at the side of the room, conscious every time he entered the university precincts of being someone. So far this was a world inviolate. Once he entered it he lived in his personal present, not the country's, allowing himself to bask in the admiring looks, the greetings, the little stir his prestige and popularity created. He was, they knew, in a class by himself. The way some of his friends drank or pursued women or smoked pot from the panwalla outside the administration building, he was addicted to his work and dazzlingly successful in it. It alone woke in him the wild sweet sensation of achievement. The thought, what am I going to do or be, argued so often among his friends and acqaintances, never occurred to him. Most students of his background had some idea, some fairly ready-made opening into employment after the degree. The greater part didn't, and even with an outstanding degree would not get decent jobs. Rishad felt separate from both groups, the privileged and the mass, when it came to his work. It ranked in its pristine purity in a category distinct from past and future. It was his one uncomplicated love, and it belonged in the present. He sharply regretted having asked the scarecrow girl to join him here. It was as stupid as if he had had bits of evidence of the past hour's assignment, glass splinters or torn cloth, sticking to him for everyone to see. He also doubted the eventual wisdom of meeting her again, though she had helped. He could not take too much for granted, even in a helper. But above all he hated this side of his life to be cluttered with the other. He did not want to talk business here in the coffee shop. He hoped she would not turn up.

In the middle of the room Madhu sat bent over her coffee cup. She had drunk it so fast it had scalded her stomach and numbed the tip of her tongue, but it had steadied her. She had gone to bed without dinner, and had eaten nothing in the morning except tea. She was eating one meal a day. Her coffee was finished but she couldn't get up and go where her brother, who had paid, waited outside. He had gone ahead to unlock his cycle. Classes were all right. Drinking coffee here was all right. Sitting in a chair in the common room at her college was all right. There was a security in being among lots of people, and she, who had been shy and had hung back and had skirted the walls of rooms so as not to attract notice, went straight to the middle of rooms, the heart of crowds, now. It was getting to and from places that paralysed her. Four days after coming home from the hospital she had run away to the university. It was the last place she wanted to go to but there was no other. She screamed in the night and at home they said she was going mad the way she carried on. The neighbourhood would soon know what had happened, already there were questions. And the only solution they could think of was marriage. They had got out her horoscope, had it read, and the pundit had told them she would get married within a year. Because she was dark and people thought her ugly, she prayed they wouldn't be able to find her a bridegroom, though the astrologer had assured them they would. She had been in terror of meeting her tormentors again, but they were known devils she could recognize and hide from, if they were still around. She couldn't from the unknown face and hands of the marriage to which they would deliver her. She wept and pleaded to be left alone but her family paid no attention. Though they didn't try to stop her going to her classes, they started looking for a husband. They put her brother in charge of her and let her go until they could hand her to another household. But Madhu was waiting for another sort of deliverance. Prayers were answered, the soiled made clean by fasting and penance, God in his mercy appeared to those in need. Her brother frowned at her from the doorway. Screwing up her courage Madhu rose from her chair and walked out of the coffee shop.

Skinny walked in when Rishad was halfway through his coffee, looking a little more substantial. She wore a purple cotton sari and a tangle of beads, and had a long plait of hair she kept forward over her right shoulder. Noticing these details for the first time, Rishad wondered if she had changed her clothes or been wearing these all the time. Not quite a woman, but less of a child, if he did not look at her thin arms and scrawny wrists. Her appearance made her sitting down at his table unremarkable. She would be taken for some raw youngster new at the university whom her parents had asked him to keep an eye on. No one would think twice about her settling like a blown leaf opposite him.

'Did anything happen after I left?' he asked.

She shook her head. 'Like what?' she said suddenly, leaning forward, a little breathless

He checked his exasperation. 'Did anyone come? Was it noticed?'

It was the kind of explicitness, putting the actual events into words, he disliked and avoided. Details were only discussed in strict privacy at group meetings.

'Oh no, it was not. I mean it couldn't be at that time, with Papa out on his rounds. And even if he'd been at home, his clinic is right the other side of the house, and if there were five earthquakes and a howling gale he wouldn't notice them once he's with his outpatients. The way he *concentrates*.'

Papa's clinic. Rishad remembered the name Dr. P.K. Jaipal on the gate on the other side of the house. Concentration was a quality he could appreciate. So the doctor, in or out of the house, would not have found the damage yet.

'What about your mother? Was she out too? And there must be servants.' He had only seen the root-vegetable himself.

She shook her head again, using a lot of energy in the little action.

'One. Servant, that is. Deaf as a doorpost. I burst a fire-cracker too near him one Divali when I was little. Papa has tried and tried to make him wear a hearing aid, but he won't.' She shrugged, her eyes all over the room as if she were at her own birthday party. 'My mother's dead. There isn't a soul in the house at this time. Bhola gets back from the bazaar around eleven and he probably won't enter any other room in the house for hours. It was a very good time to choose. They'll say –'

He cut her short. 'D'you want some coffee?'

She nodded with vigour, pausing while he ordered.

'They'll put it down to the Naxalites. That – is what you are.'

It was a statement, not a question. She was looking at him with awe.

Rishad was curt. 'I'm not and names are not important. What is important is to wipe out the mess and the misery.'

She nodded quickly, 'I know. When will we do your house?'

It took him aback.

'Your neighbourhood was chosen as a kind of – sample,' he explained, 'It doesn't mean we're going to do every house in town.'

'Oh natually not.' Her alacrity to agree disconcerted him. So did her rapt 'You've got an eighty-per-cent-average.'

'How do you know?'

'Everyone knows. It's a récord for the university. I'm doing history Honours too,' she confided, 'First year.'

'Marks are not important either,' Rishad said, consciously lofty, accustomed to tribute.

He noticed her eyes, brown and eager. Skinny Jaipal had passable eyes. The eyes were fixed unblinking on him.

'I know they aren't important – compared with the movement,' she agreed, but went back nevertheless adoring to his marks. 'You'll get a scholarship to the United States.'

'I don't want it,' he said abruptly, surprising himself.

Didn't he? He hadn't really thought about it. It belonged among plans, and he had none.

'You don't?'

'I don't know whether I do or not,' he said irritated, 'It's not relevant at the moment.'

'Oh. She was waiting with a frown for him to go on, her coffee cup held in both hands tilting dangerously, her elbows in a puddle of coffee, her saucer already filled with slop. He took her cup firmly from her and put it down. The very idea of recruiting anyone who couldn't so much as hold a cup of coffee without spilling half of it was quite idiotic. He had satisfied himself about the position at her house, and she was too much of an awe-struck infant to wish to do him any harm. He got up, scraping his chair back.

'Please!' she halted him.

She either talked non-stop or delivered these one-word appeals like commands of dire urgency.

'Well, what is it?'

'When will you tell me about the movement?'

'Not now.'

'When please?'

He was intensely irritated at the way her eyes clung famished to him. She looked fourteen. She must be about sixteen or seventeen, first year. He had to remind himself again that he must recruit followers. Here was one for the taking and, he assessed, she might after all be good material. She was certainly keen.

'All right. On Monday at three o'clock at the cemetery.'

The cemetery was on the main road, far enough away from the university.

7

'Harriet Eleanor Coleman 1795-1824 beloved wife of John James Coleman, deeply mourned by her husband and three children.' The tombstone was hot but not burning to the touch. The sky today was sullen and swollen, heavy with unshed rain, the sun furred over by a thick haze. Rishad accustomed his hand to the tombstone, trying to decide whether to sit down at its base or look for a spot protected by tree shade. The inscription though briefer than some of the others was in elaborate Gothic letters, a mark of special tribute to Harriet Eleanor, beloved wife, dead at twenty-nine. He looked around him. There wasn't this much space between living bodies in the city's crowded jhuggis or the pigmy-sized hutments where construction workers lived while they worked on a site. The cemetery was fascinating to explore, many of its tombstones of the English dead. The remains of Harriet Eleanor, far from home, were now part of Delhi, inextricably mixed with Indian clay, wind and weather, leaf mould, soil and stone.

Rishad looked up to see the girl flying toward him. She would probably trip over a stone on the uneven ground before she reached him. She threw Ancient India and a folder of notes on the grass, and herself down beside it, facing him, breathless and attentive. Her sari slipped off her shoulder and he noticed her childish breasts and the ink on her fingers.

'I thought you'd forget,' she gasped.

He had arrived at the cemetery ten minutes earlier, thankful there was no one about. Not that it would have mattered. It was about three miles from the university so no one they knew would be around to see them together. And even if they were seen she hardly counted as a person. A blown twig of a girl. But she was a loose end in this business still to be neatly tucked in so that she would not inadvertently give him away. And then again she might be recruited. All the same it was annoying to be stuck in this time-wasting appointment with her. With difficulty he recalled her name, or the name he thought of her by, Skinny Jaipal. As she had already sat herself down and was waiting for him to talk, there was no point in looking for a shadier place. He sat down too.

'What do you want to know?' he asked.

Today he had time and he decided to educate her.

'About the philosophy,' she said promptly.

'The main thing to remember is that there's no room for philosophy where there's hunger and terrible inequality. There's only room for surgery to remove them, and they have to be removed, like a cancer, like filth – he made an incisive gesture followed by her startled eyes, 'in any way at all, with any weapon. The only way that will not work is with words. There have been enough words. We have to act.'

She was sitting very upright, listening with her whole body, her nose shining. Any other girl would have suggested shifting out of the glare to a cooler spot.

'People like us,' he continued, 'who are so used to the poverty around us that we don't see it any more, can only be shocked into change. It can't come any other way.'

He could see pictures forming in her mind, giving birth to a disciple. His words – mere words, after all – did have that power then, he thought ironically. But the whole of society was not a skinny girl with chicken bones and a social conscience. He checked the surmise. How did he know who and what she was? The third injunction laid down: Don't presume your listener is with you. Test him.

'I *know*,' she said before he could, her eyebrows screwed in concentration.

'You know what?'

'That a shock is necessary. It happened to me in a flash when I started cutting up my own clothes.'

'Your own clothes?'

'Yes, yesterday. It was my first Act and there was a meaning to it, because I was doing it to myself and not to somebody else. It was like a test of my belief. Everyone should do it to themselves first, don't you think? To test themselves, don't you think?'

Skinny's eyes were looking straight into his. He felt dumb.

'Whose,' he asked reluctantly, 'were the other clothes – '

'The day you came? Those were my mother's.'

'But your mother –'

'She's dead. When I was six. But Papa kept everything of hers to give me.'

Twice-plundered Skinny Jaipal looked serene as she said it.

'Why did you help me do it?'

'I knew straightaway it was for a purpose. It was a rite. I knew straightaway who you must be.'

He sensed, unwillingly, the uncorrupted core of her, waiting to be taken, moulded, used. Such people lent great strength to a movement. He realized at the same time that anything he told her would be just words again compared with the reality of her own stern violent act. Some of the words he had planned slipped away and he spoke more earnestly, less loftily than before. He described the movement in simple general terms, its ideology, it goals. There had to be more and more recruits, he said, with a total commitment to the cause. They would be people who felt a recoil from the waste and affluence the country could not afford, hatred at the contrasts, determination that these must end. Politicians, whatever their political colour, and whatever they piously said, got fat from office. They would never banish the contrasts, never in ten thousand years build an equal society. How could they, when they were products of the rot themselves, of caste, of vested interests and stinking old ideas? It would take the young to build, and to do that they had to pledge themselves to sober, calculated destruction. There was no other way. The common people would eventually learn what was good for them, when the message spread to enough of them in the towns and the rural areas. And then they would seize their chance.

'Like Bhola Ram might about his hearing aid,' she interrupted.

Rishad looked blankly at her.

'Our cook. I *told* you about him. He doesn't even realize a hearing aid will make him hear better.'

She sighed deeply. He had not known she had that much breath in her.

'Go on,' she commanded.

Rishad picked up a stick and snapped it smartly in two.

'There's nothing to go on with,' he said irritably, 'this is not a bedtime story.'

The irony was lost on Skinny.

'Will there be a government?' she asked.

'A government?'

'After our movement succeeds.'

Oh. Yes, of course. Eventually.'

Meanwhile planned raids, attacks on chosen installations and neighbourhoods would continue, meticulously organized and delivered, arms would be collected, and the movement would spread like hot ashes blown westward, northward over the country.

'Won't it go south?'

'Of course,' he said, impatiently.

She was so literal. It had already gone south but had not made much headway except in one State. It would once the organization collected itself again and got more members. He did not tell her it was in poor shape at present. But even, he remembered, the Ramayana had gone South. A legend had travelled, making India one enduring cultural unity from the Himalayas to the sea. And again it had crossed the Vindhyas in the person of Shankaracharya. If a message could be carried in the eighth century by one barefoot monk with an intellectual passion, what could prevent another transformation under a different bible today? Today ideas could spread like fire. They *were* spreading among industrial workers who were highly organized and had leadership. It was the unorganized ones, the professions that had no unions and no political consciousness at all, who had to be worked on. His group had stopped experimenting with the rural areas. Take a time like this, when farmers who had planted their maize and rice and other crops once the monsoon had made a good beginning, now stood looking up at the tormenting sky. Long lines of grain were scorching under the gruelling sun. You'd think the farmers would be ripe for action, angry or desperate enough for it. But they weren't. They were just waiting, rooted to their patches of soil, for the rain to come. Once it did they would not care a fig for anything else. To stir, to break and rebuild that mentality was beyond him and his group. Revolution, his movement believed, was made by circumstances, not men. Then why didn't *these* circumstances produce revolt? But he did not speak to Skinny of any of this. Nor of the lengthening shadow over the movement. Armed force had been met with armed force, small contingents hunted from their hideouts and blotted up like spilled ink, prisoners in their thousands festering in chains. It was too soon to tell her any of that. And the time might never come at all. She was too much of a child.

Skinny saw the look on his face. 'Are you in danger?' she asked.

'Not really.' It was only half true, and the work had to go on.

'Can I join?'

'Perhaps later,' he said.

It sounded weak, time always intervening to delay change. Rishad picked himself off the grass, brushing it off him.

'Well, I must go,' he said.

Skinny did not stir. She was looking up at him, pleading.

'Actually I'm working for a scholarship. I love my work. I really – love my work.'

As though loving her work might be a disloyalty to the tasks he had been speaking of, as it well might be. Work had to take its place in the scheme, and its place might not be very important, depending on the job in hand. Her plea probed an ache in him.

'So do I', he said abruptly.

'Then it's all right for me to spend time on it?'

'Yes, it's all right.'

He did not know what else to say. Ideally he should have asked her to keep herself in readiness for such jobs as might come her way, though they might interfere with her work. But this twig of a girl would be better off for the time being with her studies. Her enthusiasm was good but it might be dangerous. She needed to grow up a bit more. She nodded, relieved. Suddenly she smiled. It was big and radiant. When the rest of her catches up with that smile, he found himself thinking, Skinny Jaipal will be quite a woman.

'Still,' she said, getting up and brushing off her sari, 'you can assign me some duties. I'd like that. I'd like to help.'

He wanted to retort that duties were not for him to assign nor could they be so casually handed out.

'Not yet,' he said again, 'maybe later.'

'Promise?'

In a country where hands did not so casually meet, and greeting was distant, it took him aback to find Skinny Jaipal's thin hand thrust confidently, comrade-like, toward him. He took it in a cautious clasp.

69

She gave her characteristic gasp as if she'd suddenly remembered to breathe. 'I've got to go. I've got a class, and then a dancing lesson.'

She picked up Ancient India and her notes.

'Oh listen. Will you come to the concert the "first year" are organizing? Some items are by us and some by professional musicians and the proceeds will go to the Drought Relief Fund.'

He had seen the posters on campus and had had no intention of going to anything so dull as a freshman concert.

'Oh, come please.'

'Are you taking part?'

'I'm dancing,' she said gleefully, 'Manipuri. I can keep a seat for you in the front row.'

'No,' he said hastily, 'don't do that. I'll try and come, but don't expect me.'

She shone her smile at him and rushed off as unceremoniously as she had come, her sari seeming to wrap itself round her legs as if any minute it would trip her. Rishad took a cigarette out of the pack in his pocket and walked to the shade of a tree to sit down and smoke it. It was a recent habit, experimental as most things he did were. His friends had started to smoke years earlier, one reason why he had deliberately delayed. It now gave him time to go over the meeting with Skinny. He had done the correct thing seeing her again and rounding off the untidy end. He was not worried about her. Her responses had been clean. Basically she was good material. Later she might be valuable to them and he would keep in touch with her. Her ardent sympathy would stay in bounds because she was involved with her studies. It was a long time since anyone outside the group had remotely roused his respect.

A loneliness filled him, the loneliness of not enough others to share a belief with. The people in his environment were like tribes and clans walled in by their fixed ideas, reacting in predictable blocks. His classmates never read or asked questions. Pinky and her gang were morons. Even his mother believed things should go on more or less as before. The star of her generation had been freedom, a sacred word for her. But Rishad had been born free, in a world he could not accept. He had to change it. If ever there had been a pure creation, as Harriet Eleanor and her Christian ilk believed, it had to come again. No canker of evil, a world wiped clean of private lust

70

for private gain. The teaching that right and wrong, good and evil are part of the cosmos and each man's destiny his own to work out within that cosmic pattern through all eternity might still suit the fat entrenched rich. To have forever to work out your salvation was all right if you were not hungry or desperate, if every minute did not seem an eternity. Most people couldn't live on a diet of philosophy. They needed another easier-to-grasp prescription for change.

On his motor-cycle skimming back to the university he saw in the distance ahead a familiar figure trudging along. He recognized from afar the red and green print sari, gay as a flag on the hot deserted road, the plait of hair swinging behind. He slowed down as he approached Skinny.

'Are you walking?' he asked in amazement.

Skinny wiped her sweating forehead with the end of her sari.

She said mockingly, 'Is there some other way to go? There's not a scooter in sight.' And the paucity of buses and their crowding was a sour joke at the university. What had possessed him to imagine she would arrive any way but on foot?

'I'll give you a lift.'

For the first time, Skinny looked embarrassed. 'I don't think that would be proper,' she said primly, 'And someone might see me.'

'Oh for heaven's sake, I'll drop you at a respectable distance from your college.'

'I should think so,' she said with dignity but still hung back.

She'd walked miles under a punishing sun to meet him, and ripped up her own clothes and her mother's clothes before that – hardly the conventional mould. But here she was fussing about riding pillion on his motor-cycle. Then she consulted her watch and decided of necessity to accept his offer. To his amazement she began to equip herself for a major expedition, hitching up her sari, wrapping the loose end of it around her head and shoulders, only the tip of her nose showing by the time she was done.

'Well, get on, and if you don't hang on to me, you'll fall off,' he raised his voice above the motor.

'Oh,' said Skinny, scared, 'all right.'

She hurried off with an untypically timid wave of her hand when he left her near her college.

8

'There's an Englishman coming to dinner tomorrow,' said Devi.

'Then English food,' said Kirti, adding morosely that the summer vegetables, pumpkin, marrow etc. were hideous cooked the English way.

'No, no, Indian food. But no chillies.'

What Kirti called 'English food' was a combination of flavours that added up to an uncannily tasty cuisine. How, without proper ovens and fancy aids had Indian cooks learned to make elaborate foreign creations, confections of sponge and cream, complicated decoration? When people spoke of national creativity and home-grown science, of ingenuity and talent, Devi thought of Indian cooks, of where they had come from and what they had achieved, of roads to cordon bleu travelled unremarked. Kirti's own flawless cakes in the past had been 'baked' in empty biscuit tins on a coal fire, with three glowing coals on top of the tin to provide 'oven' heat, the time they took and the temperature anybody's guess. Though the contrast between Kirti and cake had been so vast, Devi had known beyond any doubt, and regardless of any political or economic theory, that gaps such as these took neither centuries nor violent upheavals to bridge. They took Kirtis, and there were plenty of those. Now Kirti had a gas stove and cylinder and the gas flared merrily all day with a supreme disregard of its cost. Kirti understood electricity perfectly. A switch he knew had to be turned off. Gas was different and he was mutinous when she complained. As far as he was concerned, if a coal fire could be left on once it was lighted in the early morning, so could gas. Devi had to go and turn it off herself when she was home, and once or twice in anxiety about her bills she had even phoned from office about it.

'You said when freedom came we wouldn't have to bother about all these things, there'd be plenty of everything.'

'I didn't say anything of the sort.' But she was resigned to the shortcomings of 'freedom' being regularly laid at her door.

'Now that Shivraj is dead, what's going to become of us?' said Kirti suddenly.

'What do you mean? Everything is going on as before.'

Kirti grunted. 'Seems there's plenty of trouble. This closed and that closed. Rishad hasn't been to university for the past week.'

'It'll open next Monday,' said Devi.

'Maybe', said Kirti, 'and maybe not. When was it closed in Shivraj's time? And you should hear the talk in the bazaar. You said when freedom came – '

'About tomorrow's dinner,' Devi interrupted.

Normally bazaar talk interested her hugely. Today it threatened to revolve around 'you said when freedom came'.

'Who else is coming?'

'Usman Sahib and his begum. Perhaps one other person.'

'Who?'

'I'm not sure. Rishad might ask a friend of his.'

Trying to include a friend of Rishad's was like the Cabinet's paper Plan, a non-starter. Rishad must *have* some friends, but where they were and what he did about them she had no idea. A home should be a meeting place of generations. That was one of the warming things about the Puri home and probably every other home in Delhi except hers.

Kirti told her his menu for the Englishman's dinner and that he would make something cold to start with, a mousse, and for the sweet – Devi and Kirti looked out of the window at the same instant that Rishad's joyous shout came from the front verandah, 'Mum, it's raining!' 'We'll see how long,' muttered Kirti, while she went out to join Rishad and watch the fine shy needle-slant straighten into a vigorous pour. Ajaib Singh came round the corner from the garage, oblivious of them, his turban off, his long hair streaming down his back, both hands rubbing his head and arms, his face and beard uplifted to catch the downpour. Even Kirti appeared in the doorway armed with a kitchen knife, peered out with narrowed eyes, conceded 'It'll last' and went indoors again.

'You said when freedom came the monsoon would be regular'

73

Rishad raised his voice above the gathering turbulence in imitation of Kirti, and Devi and her son laughing, settled down in cane chairs to watch the unbelievable rain.

Well, they *had* talked about freedom so much. Its absence, its coming, what they would do with it when it came. Her growing up, her career, her whole life had been ordered by the freedom to come. The early Christians must have felt that imminence about the second coming. Yet, to Rishad born and brought up in that atmosphere, it meant no more than pre-history. It *was* pre-history, an event whose antiquity had no relation to the present and with which he had no ties — no ties even with something as hard-won as the battles she herself had fought. When he said 'India' he meant something different.

Rain billowing into the dug-up flower beds bordering the lawn filled them with rich puddles. It sprayed the verandah and soaked the edges of her sari. She drew it over her ankles and taking her feet out of their slippers, let the cool water sprinkle them. Earth scents and earth colours rose in splendour around her. When Rishad said, 'I can't stand Pinky's family' he meant no personal dislike, he meant class. And Rishad did not want to know anyone who disagreed with him.

She went to her room, touching her son's head briefly. Tomorrow Michael would be here, before her mind was ready to receive the fact. Her mind and facts, uppermost all day, took a back seat as she sat down at her dressing table and looked at herself in the mirror. The dressing table was one of Shivraj's presents to her. Bright brown Kashmiri walnut, carved in slender curves by an unerring hand, it was the work of some unknown craftsman who knew in his bones what beauty was. It had a cameo-like delicacy against the staid ugly background of P.W.D. furniture in the rest of the house. She adjusted the two oval side mirrors to see herself in profile, pushing her hair back from her face. A Rumanian sculptor who had done a head of Shivraj had studied her face during his carrot juice intervals and declared it was not for sculpture. No bones, no scars, no hollows, no crevices, no lines, no *accumulation*, he had gestured with feeling, as though he were examining rock and cliff formations or volcanoes and craters, and was pained by the dismal fallout the

74

last eruption had disgorged. For his purposes, no face. 'My dear Excellency,' he had told Shivraj, 'not for sculpture.' She would be better painted, with that texture of skin and its *continuousness* – a ruling texture, so that one almost overlooked her features. One almost did not see them.

'Pity about your features,' Shivraj had plagued her after that.

'You've dealt a terrible blow to a vain woman like my sister,' he had told Jaroslav, 'Here she was thinking she was Nefertiti. What about her eyes, or do those get overlooked too?'

'Ah those.' Jaroslav frowned, examining them. 'Those she has, Width and corners. But better painted.'

They had talked about faces that could be graven in stone or bronze, others like hers that couldn't. The passing light affected them, or a breeze.

'A flicker can change it,' said Jaroslav, 'Nefertiti no.'

Today's light and breeze were suiting her face, giving it the sheen her superb health always highlighted. But Jaroslav might have condescended to do her now that politics had claimed and marked her. Fine lines on her forehead, something perceptibly different about the set of her mouth, end-of-the-day eyes. Sometimes they looked that at the start of the day too. A subject for sculpture, less so for a mirror now. She wished she could hand herself into expert care as other women she knew did, and have signs of middle age tucked out of sight.

Jaroslav had been a delightful companion, talking to them of contemporary European art, a subject that did not normally cross their path. So many subjects didn't, submerged as they were by a veritable haemorrhage of the here and now. 'There is no human being on earth as ignorant and uncultured as the professional politician,' Shivraj had remarked, 'I'll have to give up this office so that I can read a book once in a while.' Even their times together were few and far between by then, a great personal loss to her. Michael had not understood when he quarrelled so fiercely with her that Shivraj was both rest and excitement, new and familiar, longing and fulfilment, and, for her, the way men would be aeons hence, when the planet evolved a finer breed. Once he became the country's she had had to wait for him. Unlike earlier, when she'd been able to argue him into an outing, when they had got into the car because the day sparkled and she at the wheel had swung it out toward the river, toward freedom and salvation. They had carried lunch and spent the afternoon in their boat and had known as if a clock had struck, the exact second when the apricot light would drain upward, as though a giant breath had sucked it up, and chill make the river rough and angular, pushing it into ridges as it tilted under the wind. She and Shivraj, motor switched off, would lie in the boat under her white woollen shawl. Borne along by the deep-flowing current, they talked in murmurs or not at all, the sky of a continent above them, thousands of miles between its borders, seas carrying ships beyond; and he would talk mostly of jail and its confines, tell her how he had dreamed of space, how he had watched the sky in all its moods, clung famished to the tree, ancient and dusty, symbol of other trees, in the prison yard, loved and yearned for the sound each living thing made, the singing of a bird, crickets and croaking night insects, the almost noiseless lizards on the barrack walls. Devi's tears had made wet diagonal paths down her cheeks, and she had been glad, glad that today she had given him the sky and the world beneath it.

She went to the window and leaned her elbows on the sill. Below her, moss patched the brick wall and a deepening puddle grew frantic with rain. She could see tiny fast things flick and glide in it and a frog immobile in a trance on its edge. A pale pure light glimmered beyond the curtain of rain, replenishing her awareness of the evening, but it was a distant troubled awareness, of things happening around her she could not control.

Kirti coughed in the doorway. 'The sweet', he reminded her and informed her he was going to make 'khir' for the Englishman's dinner. Not ten tons, she hoped. Kirti loathed economy. Michael was coming to dinner tomorrow. She had been, as far as he knew, a few years older than himself, a woman of thirty-four, when they met. He didn't know she had been seventeen in her avidity and sheltered inexperience – a woman who had married, borne a child and been widowed all within four years, the rest of her expended on Shivraj. She had taken Michael with the candour, innocence and appetite of a seventeen-year-old, in incongruous command of the situation, made imperious by her need. It might have ended that way, but then he had become part of the intimate gathering around Shivraj, and there had been no escape.

At five to eight next evening Devi, who had been dictating a complicated letter to her evening P.A., did not hear a taxi drive up. Anand was cheerful, young and appallingly careless, with an M.A. in English that did not rise to spelling and punctuation. She had to go laboriously with him. Pause, long pause, comma, two m's in immediate and so on.

'Please be careful about addressing it,' she told him, 'It's the Society for the Promotion, not prevention, of English. I don't want a language agitation on my hands.'

Anand chuckled, 'As if.'

She found Michael in the kitchen, lifting lids off saucepans. Kirti, putting finishing touches to an elegant mousse, said accusingly without looking up, 'You never told me it was him.' Michael's kiss was warm against her temple. She took him to the verandah behind the house where potted plants made a cool green jungle at either end, and a single black-branched tree dripped and shivered in the breeze on the small back lawn. A low growl of thunder announced more rain. In the murmuring dark Michael stood, a heavier greying version of himself, ten years vanished trace unseen between them. He seemed uncertain what to do with the bottle of Scotch he was carrying, looking for a surface to put it down on while he answered her questions about his flight. Anand, entrusted with putting out small tables, had forgotten to do so, and was cheerfully cycling home by now. And by the time tables were brought, Usman and Nadira had arrived. Usman and Michael embraced like long-lost brothers and started a string of questions and incomplete answers, Michael exclaiming over Usman's armsling, that delayed by several minutes his introduction to Nadira. The injury to Usman's left eye had permanently narrowed it, giving him a sinister look, and he walked with a slight limp. And finally came Rishad, touchingly beautiful in white pyjama-kurta, a lock of hair falling over his forehead. Unexpectedly Rishad took charge, treating his mother and her guests with charming ceremony, helping Michael and Nadira to whisky but taking lemonade himself.

'For you, Mum?' he enquired, holding up Michael's bottle.

'All right', she said, ' a little, in honour of Michael.'

Michael noticed she held the glass her son gave her as though it might explode, the way women who were unaccustomed to whisky treated it, like something suspicious and subvertive. Lydia had had a theory it would ruin her facial muscles. It was not fair that Devi looked as she did, in a curious way still in possession of her youth, though tired. He was intrigued once again by her complete autonomy, which far from showing any cracks or crevices, graced her like a visible ornament. She was now treating the party around her like a child on its own, free to flourish without smothering care.

Rishad talked to Michael with ease and knowledge about Left Wing politics in Britain and the Left Wing phenomenon all over the world, and made Michael laugh by asking had the Soviet Union or the London School of Economics influenced Indian Communists more? Devi looked on fascinated. The adamant hard-liner, principles to the ready. I will and I won't. And then this transformed other, performing a conventional duty with grace, as he easily might not have done on another evening. Just sat there, politely indifferent, or being aloof when spoken to. Tonight he was taking the trouble to really talk, exhibiting his own reading and thinking so that Michael, she could see, was enchanted. Usman who knew Rishad well was enjoying him too, while Nadira never needed to do anything but look herself, black lashes curving against her cheek. A lotus in a lake, detached from the land. And she looked most detached when she was most threatened. Nadira was not here this evening, Devi noted. She never was, except as a physical presence, and not that either when they had foregathered with Shivraj.

By the time they had eaten it was raining hard. They sat in the drawing room, Usman talking of the dangers of boredom and how they were affecting the university. A contagious disease spreading its tentacles into the very vitals of the system. The Hindus particularly were a frighteningly bored lot. What else could they be when nothing new had entered their mental orbit for hundreds of years?

'They'll storm into buildings, stab and rape on campus and kill Vice-Chancellors because they're so bored. I can't say I entirely blame them,' he added thoughtfully.

'Killing out of boredom?' Michael demurred.

'Well, a Hindu can kill without a qualm,' Usman amended, 'so long as he stays detached from the action. Isn't that what the Battle of Kurukshetra is all about? Read the Bhagavad Gita, Michael.'

Devi said his argument was a piece of sophist nonsense, but it had, as Usman liked to do, provoked Michael to discussion. Rishad, sitting on the floor in the middle of the room, looked alert, but had relapsed into silence. Nadira's hands clasping and unclasping in her lap gave the impression that she was going through an ordeal with rapidly vanishing composure.

'That idea is not confined to Hinduism,' said Michael, 'Islam has its "jehad", Christianity the "good fight" that must be fought, where "Christ is thy strength and Christ thy right". How are they different from Kurukshetra?'

'The difference is your religion and mine don't make a virtue of non-violence. It's these Hindus,' his hand swept over Depi and Rishad, 'who need to know what they stand for. This Trimurti business, three faces to every action, will be the ruin of this country, and look what passes for modernity among them – ' His grey eyes looked disdainful as he studied Devi, 'Deep down this poor misguided woman believes – oh undoubtedly she believes – her blood is purer than someone else's because of the accident of her caste. She may even think she's superior because her skin is a shade fairer than the next person's. Could ignorance, or is it arrogance, go much further?'

Because Nadira had spoken so little, fathoms deep in her remoteness, Devi turned to ask her about her children and to get a bright smile and a polite adequate response before she became quiet again.

Usman stirred restlessly in his chair and went on. 'A Hindu remedy has to be found to all this. I am sitting here with a damaged eye and by the sheerest chance no cracked skull, because we haven't been able to find a remedy. And since no Hindu in this land of ours has come up with one, I'll have to.'

'How is your eye now?' asked Devi to change the subject, while she groped for the meaning of what he was saying.

'Healed. But it's a blessing it happened. The urgency of the situation wouldn't have reached me otherwise.'

'You've been aware of it almost since you took over. It's all down in your paper.'

79

'On paper. And papers can always wait. This can't. I knew that with absolute certainty when that cyclone hit my room.'

'It was blackmail through violence,' Nadira began in a low voice, 'nothing more than that. You've got to have the police on campus to see that it doesn't happen again.'

'So I have to get into action myself,' Usman cut in smoothly as if she had not spoken.

'Where have we gone wrong, what have we failed to see that we saw before?' he spoke wonderingly.

'Another attack like that and I shall be widowed,' said Nadira sharply.

Extraordinary how Usman at such times paid no more attention to Nadira than if she had not been there. He went on talking relentlessly. He's working up something new, worried Devi, getting ready for battle and one of these days it is going to rock us both. Usman's eyes met and held hers compellingly. Events at the university had affected him deeply, a sign of impending crisis in him, and in the past Usman had come out of each crisis in his thinking with something fundamentally altered. It was eleven o'clock and Rishad and Nadira were making moves to get up. Usman and Michael had not stirred. They were oblivious of the time, making up for the years in between, talking avidly about power and purity.

Usman said, 'If you want to be pure, you can't run a government – though Shivraj did work to establish the nearest thing to a republic of virtue. There's not even a pretence at it now. The great and growing power of the state threatens to engulf us. We'll never be properly self-governing in this country until we vest power in little units, in people at the base.'

When she had a chance Devi said reluctantly, conscious of Nadira, 'I've an early meeting tomorrow.'

Usman got up, deliberately unhurried, and stood leaning against the mantlepiece while Nadira said her goodbyes. He then said his own, lingering in a manner purely formal and courteous with Devi before she accompanied them out to the entrance. Nadira, looking on, wondered how he could, without going near a woman, *this* woman, look as if he possessed her utterly, a latent sensuality about even this ordinary leave-taking. It was the intangibles in her life with Usman that tormented her, nothing so explicable as adultery, though that was one of her demons too. What bound these people together, even when one of them was dead?

Later, undressing in front of the long mirror in their bedroom, she remarked, 'I don't know why you hate admitting it. They attacked you because you're a Muslim. You should never have accepted this post. You didn't even want to.'

The long drive home had been cool because of the rain but indoors it was suffocatingly hot and steamy. He closed the doors and windows and turned on the air-conditioner. Even this distinguished him from *them*. He sat down to anticipate the cool, his face and thoughts withdrawn.

'What made you accept it in the end?'

Usman did not answer. If Nadira could have seen their faces, faces he had lived with every waking moment since that day, faces that had closed in on him, looking through him, past him, settling on him for vengeance because he was, conveniently, there. Already in imagination he was with them, his soul seared by that no man's land of the young into which they had given him one savage glimpse. Their plight was frightening because it was mostly future. And to be stranded in hordes was no less frightening than to be alone. Answers must be found to an education with no moorings in its own culture, but before that, another answer, some leap forward by instinct that would create the atmosphere for the rest of the journey. He was more and more convinced he would create it, turn the tide, by stepping out among them, blurring the frontier between the teacher and the taught. That would be the beginning of trust and beyond it only good could happen. He wished he could convey this to Nadira for whom religion was the frontier, an uncrossable one, all blood-letting its cause.

'*She* wanted you to. Isn't that the reason?'

Nadira never used Devi's name.

'Partly.'

'Well this is the result. This university doesn't want a Muslim in charge. You shouldn't have been talked into it.'

'Being a Muslim has nothing to do with it. The Vice-Chancellor of Jadhavpur was stabbed eight months ago. He was a Hindu.'

'I never set foot on the campus any more. I'm afraid of what might happen.'

'You should come. You are much missed. I've told you so before. And the poetry circle you started for the faculty wives is languishing.'

She had been a sensation when she first started it, but once the adulation settled down she had not been as interested.

'It was a terrible mistake to stay in this country,' said Nadira.

Usman, in the act of lighting a cigarette, crushed it unlit into the ashtray. He said coldly, 'This is my country. Where else do you want me to live?'

'It isn't mine,' she flashed.

'You chose to marry me.'

'We could have left. We could still leave. I know you don't want to go to Pakistan, but we could live abroad somewhere.'

Usman controlled his temper. It was too late at night for a scene.

'You've been caught in a trap all your life,' she said, 'The fatal charm of Shivraj — is that any reason to remain here now? He's dead. And what did you ever get from him while he was alive?'

Usman felt a fury rising in his breast.

'I did not stay here because of Shivraj. I stayed here because this is where I was born and my forefathers before me — and yours, too, I have no intention of leaving my country at this time of my life.'

She turned around, her eyes with their look of more than childlike defencelessness, a creature for slaughter and sacrifice. Either that or a prized possession. In any case, womankind, not woman. Her nightgown, the texture of fine white sugar, was moulded to her, its ribbons unfastened at her breast.

'There's no need to be so touchy. All I'm saying is there's hostility around you. I can feel it. So would you if you had any sense.'

He said with slow emphasis, 'If there's hostility, as you say, then hostility like that can only be embraced if it's to be overcome. Try to understand that.'

Nadira went to him, her fingers interlacing behind his neck.

'I don't understand that sort of statement, but never mind.'

He disengaged her arms, 'It's late. Let's go to sleep.'

'I was ready to leave the party long ago. You wouldn't get up. She has that effect on you.'

He undressed, washed and got into bed. The interval did not sever the thread of Nadira's conversation.

'Wasn't this man her lover at one time? What does she have that's so special? More of the Shivraj magic? I've never been able to understand Shivraj's hold on you. What was it?'

Lying on his back Usman stared up into the still warm velvet dark and said softly, 'Love and friendship'

What was anyone's hold on anyone but that? He had never made his friendship with Shivraj a stepping ladder to fame or fortune. It would have revolted him to advance himself in that manner and he had refused each opening Shivraj had offered him, preferring to go his own distinguished way unassisted by official glitter and glamour. He had told Shivraj banteringly, 'If it's the minorities you want to do right by, there are a lot of other Muslims you can pin deco-rations on and stuff into important jobs.' Then he had added serious-ly, 'There should be one man of your acquaintance who does not profit in the remotest way by knowing you.'

'I'm not offering you anything you don't richly deserve,' Shivraj had said.

'I know. Modesty isn't one of my virtues. But I want it like this. Between you and me there should never be any but the purest coinage.'

Words like love, honour, purity, the soul's surmise, could be used with Shivraj. Shivraj had been visibly moved and had not offered Usman another opening. And in his chosen aloofness from the power structure Usman had acquired a growing moral stature and some of the unsought authority that went with it. After Shivraj's death Devi had come to him with the Vice-Chancellorship of Delhi University. A crown of thorns, she had called it, not a prize. And he had still refused.

Devi had pleaded, knowing his views, 'It's different now, Usman. I never thought I would join a government. Now it's an opportunity to be constructive, to do something – ' her voice had trailed off. He mistrusted the argument. He didn't belong to the breed that needed power in order to do things. Sometimes he felt he came from infi-nitely older, deeper roots in the soil than even Shivraj, the acclaimed hero with the much-vaunted ancestry. Usman hankered for a village past, for another form of government, one that didn't build up and up into a formidable state apparatus. His would build down, with maximum power to the small community. How else, in India, would exhausted resources, human and natural, ever recover their strength?

'From what I can see, you're offering me a policeman's job. That's what it is these days, keeping law and order on campus. I'm a teacher.'

'I know,' she said gently, 'But I need your help.'

Forlorn in mourning, her chalk-white sari and her strained face were alien negative aspects of her as she sat with him in his study refusing the tea Nadira had sent in. He had thought about it for eight days – she had given him till her return from a tour in the south – though he had known categorically from the start that he did not want the job and would take it, because Devi needed him. There were worse, more hypocritical reasons for taking on a crown of thorns. He had no doubt he had made the correct decision, though at every turn he had run into a political stranglehold. This university was under the direct control of the central government.

Nadira said from her bed, 'Why do we have to have this table between us?'

'It's your house,' he told her.

'I've been wanting to rearrange the room. I'll do it tomorrow.'

He understood her objection perfectly. He would never have allowed the table himself. It had come up by itself like other barriers between him and Nadira. He wondered what he had so incalculably roused in her that his physical attentions sharpened instead of assuaging? She mistook his loyalties for hot-blooded fantasies, the witchcraft of another woman's spell, the blaze and heat of sexual magnetism – when they were vastly simpler. The Christian scripture understood the idea perfectly when it prayed 'Give us this day our daily bread.' Man speaking to God. But it was a need between men, the true substance of brotherhood. And most precious between man and woman, stuff of the real, un-magic relationship. Bread, the necessity, the satisfaction, the miracle, the food of every day. Nadira came into his bed. Her hand moved over his bare chest and stomach. She turned his face toward her. Another pattern was added to the mosaic of reunion and resentment between them, as he gave his undivided attention to the woman beside him.

Michael walked restlessly round the room as Devi went to see her guests off. From London's wintry summer to the rousing heat of Delhi was a stimulating change. He felt sleepy but exhilarated. Devi's P.A. had received him at the small, unready-for jumbos airport, sailed him through customs while the less lucky waited interminably for clearance. He had got home to find the servant Devi had engaged waiting for him, and his rooms filled with greenery she had sent. He had unpacked his suitcase and papers. He had not slept on the plane and was deciding whether to take a short nap when a piercing shriek nearby startled him. It was followed by a high nasal whine. It was the latest movie hit, his young servant told him, being played through a loudspeaker on the corner. 'There's a wedding in that house. It's wedding season,' he explained happily. Loud braying music soon flooded the neighbourhood. As Michael showered and changed he imagined the ghosts he had lived with coming out of their cramped corners before many days had passed, breathing, stretching and sitting down pleasantly to keep him company while he went on with his book. The helpless angry turmoil that had marked the end of his affair with Devi seemed far away. That is what he had thought until he saw Devi. He had noticed first that her sari was fine cotton, looking like fluid ivory on her. The palla had slipped down her bare arm and he could see the shape of her arm through it. He had had the impression of cool purity, a body wearing the least it needed with casual grace. She had always suffered from the heat. She was carrying a pencil she had forgotten to put down. And then he had looked at her face, her eyes almost purple in the kitchen light. Meeting her had not been simple and talking to Usman had probed nerve ends, making him sharply nostalgic for the past.

They – Usman and Devi – had not so much sat at Shivraj's feet as around him, a charmed inner circle to which Michael, a latecomer and the youngest, had been admitted. He had walked into their company unawares and become an addict. Long after he left India he still hankered after the sensation his encounters with these three had woken in him. With them he entered light and warmth, an atmosphere where feelings were ardent and arguments reached heights never before scaled. They were friends who lived on each other, their lives continually touching as if they could not have enough of each other's company. Devi had a way of withdrawing from the talk, and sitting entranced and expectant, her chin resting in her hand, listening to the word duels between her brother and Usman as though they transported her to some sun-flooded summit. She looked unutterably desirable to Michael in her absorption, vibrant in every pore. Alone with her after these sessions, he had always been overcome by the surge of her emotional response, a symphony he had only partially aroused. She was a creature of her atmosphere, in a way of these two men. Fresh from them, her body was an acutely sensitive instrument so pitched that it responded by itself, to his barest touch, hardly needing the experienced and imaginative lover he was becoming. There was a splendour about loving her at these times, mysteriously connected with the other two to whom she was so close.

When Devi came back into the room and he could focus on her properly for the first time it did not take him long to see she had an air of strain about her. No loss of poise but she looked as though her being were off-centre. And there was an inwardness she had not had before. She sat down leaving a small space between them on the sofa and appealed as he moved nearer, 'Don't, Michael. You don't realize what it is to live alone so long.' He took her hand, turned it over, stroking the palm with his thumb.

She said, 'I don't quite believe you're here. Tell me about yourself.'

He put the ten years into sentences, suprising himself with the lesser person he emerged. Until this moment he had thought rather well of himself.

'Yes, I'd heard,' said Devi, 'but how could you get married *twice*?'

'It happened. I was rather happy with Nell. She wasn't with me.'

'I don't wonder. I can see it.' She gave him her other hand. 'Do this one too.'

'This is not a therapeutic massage,' objected Michael.

'That's what it is, and what you are. God, it's so long since I've been able to just sit. But apart from all these marriages, how are you? Content?'

Michael laughed. 'Compared with the last time we met?'

Her change of expression informed him she had not forgotten the dismal day, the numb silence after everything had been said. She had looked drained, as though it had needed all her determination to get up and leave his hotel room.

'Where did you go when you left my room?'

'I went home, I lay down and fell asleep from sheer emotional exhaustion. When I woke it was dark and Shivraj was in the room. He came and sat near me and I started telling him about us.'

'What did he say?'

'I'd never talked about us before but he seemed to know. He urged me, like a command, to "be happy." He'd never had a purely personal life and to him it was a priceless possession. In some ways he lived through me.'

'But you'd made your decision and you didn't regret it'. It was a statement, not a question. Devi had been so categorical about breaking with him.

Devi took her hands from him and leaned back. 'Oh Michael. Of course I had regrets. But I was obeying something deeper. It was stronger than loving you.'

Could he have obeyed 'something deeper' and what would it have been? Since they had parted, king and country, love and marriage, God and all that had followed each other down various blind alleys where they lay like used toys, all the colour gone. When there were no rules to go by you could only obey yourself. But when he'd first known her it had been a rule-riddled world and he had ignored it for need of her. Love, as far as he was concerned, had nothing to do with anything but love. With Devi he'd learned to measure even her emotion against a different, older set of values.

'You're tired. I won't keep you.' He leaned forward and kissed her gently on the lips.

Her car took him home and he was suddenly wide awake. Questions crowded his mind, partly roused by his conversation with Usman. He got out his manuscript, read a few pages of it, and sat staring at the wall in his new study trying mentally to close the unsatisfactory gaps he was now aware of in it. He got up and went to the window. The wedding celebration had been in swing for hours, neon lights blinking off and on from the hedge and trees in the corner garden, loud filmland music zigzagging through the neighbourhood. Suddenly the loudspeaker stuttered and stopped and silence descended on his part of Delhi.

9

Michael phoned next morning. 'When do we meet?'

'I forgot to give you an invitation from Veena Puri for this evening. Do you remember her?'

'Fat and gorgeous,' said Michael promptly.

'Yes. They're having a singer and buffet supper. You may meet a lot of people you know.'

'I'd love to come.'

At the party Michael was immediately carried away on a wave of celebrity by Veena and disappeared among her guests. Devi had forgotten how uncomplicated he was, easily assimilable in a mixed crowd, no strains and pulls about him. Usman and she, herself, were very much more complex. Usman could be broody and difficult. She heard Vijay's roar, amiable thunder, saw his hand clap Michael's shoulder to free him from a discussion and propel him to another part of the room. Later Devi heard Veena say to him, 'There must be so many people you know here.' And Michael reply, 'I used to but I'm very out of touch. A writer either knows hundreds of people or practically none. I belong to the latter category.'

'I don't believe it,' said Veena, 'All those books Devi tells me you've written.'

It was one of Veena's endearing qualities that she did not pretend she had read books she hadn't. After the Schoolgirl adventure series she had lapsed contentedly to women's magazines. Vijay's reading, when Devi first met him, had consisted of a magazine called Automotive Engineering. Now he read a newspaper too. Adult illiteracy of a kind. There was a tiny human filling sandwiched between the great majority below and the thin skim above, who in the course of a lifetime acquired and practised the skill known as reading. She marvelled at the ambition of trying to reach this country through the written word, instead of through some form of expression more natural to it. People sat up all night watching dance recitals and theatre, went in crowds to listen to whatever came their way, from religious recitation to political speeches. It was reading most of them couldn't do, or didn't want to even if they could. She remembered what she had to ask Rishad and went into the room where the singer was performing. After an hour of warming up, exhibiting his vocal wizardry, the artist, before getting into his magical stride for the evening, was taking a rest. Rishad had come because of the music and was sitting on the carpet with the others, managing to look unconcerned that a quartet of girls had settled like butterflies around him. Devi picking her way through the people on the floor, bent to say in his ear, 'Do any of your friends sing or dance?' He looked up frowning, 'Haven't the faintest idea. But I'll ask around. Yes, there's one.'

'Could I meet him-her-it fairly soon?'

'What for?'

'A project I have', said Devi.

'A *government* thing?' he said rudely.

'Let me, please, meet this individual.'

'All right.'

The British High Commissioner, a lean tall haggard bachelor, his knees jammed at a ten past ten angle, caught Devi's sympathetic eye and rose, snapping and cracking with the effort. Devi's sympathy extended beyond his knees. She knew, from dinner table talk at her house and his, how he yearned for Europe, the Common Market and the Nine. Sir Humphrey Scott had never been in India before, nor had any member of his family. India to him was just another foreign, very foreign country. He gratefully accepted a glass of whisky from Devi in the next room. Because of his nationality, Devi was continually assuming a base of understanding with him that wasn't there. She had to remind herself they were not somehow connected, quarrelling friends or friendly high-principled enemies. In fact there was no love or hate or even memory between them, as far as Sir Humphrey knew.

'Amazing performance,' said Sir Humphrey, revived, 'really amazing. I didn't know there were so many notes in the musical scale, or variations on them. And what a voice. Combination of music and acrobatics.'

'He was just warming up. He'll be in his element around

midnight.'

'Really?' said Sir Humphrey doubtfully, glancing down at his watch.

Michael was obviously attractive to females. Pinky, ravishing in sea green and pearls, was dancing attendance on him and he was being followed around by a girl with long lank brown hair in a long lank brown dress without a bra.

'Now who is that?' said Sir Humphrey, referring to Michael.

Devi told him.

'Ah yes. He's writing a biography about your brother.'

'A book about him,' corrected Devi, 'The official biography is being written here.' She hoped she would recognize Shivraj when the official biographer had done with him.

'Yes indeed. I was here, as you know, when your brother died, and so many of us suspected the worst would happen, if you'll forgive my saying so, without him. You know, the leader goes and everything changes, or even falls apart. It's amazing how smoothly it went here and with the Prime Minister now doing such a remarkable job.'

'Yes,' said Devi.

What Rishad and Michael had called the Left Wing phenomenon understood so clearly a fuzzy emotional egalitarianism backed by force, or threat of force, but had no understanding of the bigger slower human process of a struggle that learns through its own experience.

Veena invited them to the buffet and Devi saw Michael at one end of it, loading his plate.

'What's the occasion for this party?' Devi asked Veena, 'Have I forgotten anyone's birthday '

'Arvind is in town. He can't come often. And he's such a dear boy.'

A son-in-law was sacrosanct. God took second place. Sons-in-law who had driven their wives' relations to drink, desperation and bankruptcy, somehow vanished blameless into the family's annals.

'I hope he'll stay a dear boy,' said Devi, risking displeasure.

'What a thing to say. *Look* at him.'

Devi looked. Neat pudgy Arvind was placing plump white pieces of chicken on the little hill of rice on his plate. He looked up and saw Devi. 'Hello Aunty. Let me help you.' And when she said she would help herself he strolled off to a corner of the room to eat. Pinky was fluttering around looking after her mother's guests. Devi remembered the weeks of her engagement to Ishwar, when her hand seemed to have grown into his and felt cold and empty without his; Shivraj laughing, 'He won't run away if you let go of his hand'; herself replying with passionate energy, 'He *will*'. She had known in her bones it wouldn't last. Good people, tender people, those you worshipped because they had a curious untouched innocence about them, did the unforgivable thing of dying. They went away beautifully unblemished and left you to struggle and cope.

'Go and sit with Michael,' said Veena 'He's at one of the tables along the verandah.'

'What role does an ambassador have these days?' asked Michael when she joined him, 'with special envoys rushing around to sort out problems?'

'An ambassador lives in an embassy,' said Devi, 'and in Delhi that's like a visit to another planet, where everything *works*, air-conditioners, lights, water. Not to mention powerful attractions for the local populace like Scotch and wine.'

'I begin to see his importance. What's this one like?'

'Nice. And lost. He's the join between two eras. With him you know it's over once and for all, the last 200-odd years we shared. Do you always eat so much, Michael?'

'Usually. Why?' asked Michael with his mouth full.

'Then everyone in the West doesn't count calories.'

'They count whatever they're told to count. I'm certain the potato is going to make a dramatic comeback soon as the new miracle food. They'll all be grabbing potatoes then.'

Veena was making distress signals from the doorway. 'Michael, you haven't taken any of the fish. I insist you come and get more to eat.'

Michael waved and promised and gave Devi a smug look. He had changed, apart from putting on weight. He had an assurance he had not had before, a quality not to be manipulated. Since their last meeting he had written three what the reviewers called major biographies and lived lives she knew nothing of. He apparently had the same kind of thought.

'I've filled in at least one gap since I arrived,' he said.

'What was that?'

'Rishad. I'd been thinking of him as a child now grown up. But one doesn't realize how much happens with the passage of years. He's quite a person.'

'Yes he is.'

The mixture of pride and hesitation in her voice prompted him to say, 'Talent makes problems. But he's got solid interests and they should help. I saw him in the music room just now engrossed in the performance, not noticing anything around him.'

'He's likely to sit there all night, forgetting to eat. He used to play the sitar himself but he's given it up. He seems to have given up his friends too.'

The girl without the bra came up to their table with her plate, said, 'May I join you?' and joined them, her metallic earrings dangling against her cheeks. She did not look much older than Rishad and she plunged into a vigorous attack on one of Michael's biographies. Michael, who had got up to help disentangle the girl's long skirt from the chair as she sat down, listened with interest to her charges and gave her long considered replies, till she left at a signal from one of her friends.

'Who is she?' asked Devi.

'I have no idea. She's trying to discover too many things all at once but she'll discover some in the process, which is better than what Usman was saying last night about boredom and no outlets. That's explosive stuff. What outlet is there, for instance, for Rishad?'

'I don't know. What would you do in his place?'

Michael reflected. 'I think I would act – in some direction. He has definite views and they don't make for an armchair existence. I'd say he's actively involved – in something.'

A golden mountain of spun sugar masking buried layers of cream and fruit arrived at their table. Michael helped himself after Devi refused.

'Devi, how did Shivraj die?'

'How?'

'Yes. Did he fall ill?'

'No, but he was never in good health after his last imprisonment.

92

He had to be careful about over-exerting himself, and he wasn't careful. Nor did he have checkups.'

'And you were with him all the time?'

'No,' she said, 'he was away from Delhi so much, and so was I. What are you trying to say, that he came to some harm?'

'I'm not sure what I'm trying to say, perhaps just that there is more than one way to kill a man. Or that a man like Shivraj could die if through one crucial error of judgement he let the reins slip and the direction change. A change of this sort here could reverse a whole tide, undo what Shivraj had done, maybe his life's work. As easily as undoing knitting. Pull out one stitch and the rest rips out. No one knew that better than Shivraj.' Michael took out a packet of cigarettes and offered one to Devi, who shook her head, intent on his words. 'I remember asking him once what he wanted most. He said, "A long life." Well, that's natural enough, but he wanted mainly to live long enough for free institutions to become part of the soil, become a way of life and thinking that no future could destroy.'

Devi, one hand against her forehead, as though it ached, said, 'Yes, he wanted that.'

'According to Usman all that welding is being taken apart, with great care and much egalitarian fanfare, in preparation for something quite different. What were the signs before he died?'

She said, 'I'll have that cigarette after all, Michael,' and waited for him to light it. She recalled, weighing each word for accuracy, 'They were crowding him, this group that's in now, for some time before he died, bringing pressure –'

'What kind of pressure?'

'Threatening to divide the Party, go their own way and make trouble, and I know he was under a strain. They wanted to get more of their own men into Party positions and the Cabinet, to "speed up the revolution", as they called it.'

'Did they succeed?'

'No, Shivraj didn't trust them. Except,' she indicated a table further along the verandah, 'Minerals and Metals. Shivraj took him in as a compromise to avoid a rupture in the Party and also because he thought this one was all right, good material for training.'

Michael followed her glance. A man in a batik print bush shirt, a politician who unlike many others Michael had met here as a journalist, had the social graces and an articulate tongue, judging by the attention he was commanding so easily at his table.

'How right is Usman in his assessment?' he asked Devi.

'Usman is –,' she stopped to put it succinctly, 'free. He thinks. So one has to pay some attention to what he says.'

Michael nodded slowly.

'And he gives me courage,' she added, 'Michael, it's such a relief to be talking like this'

'If you can bear to leave the party, let's go to my place,' said Michael.

'I can bear it. Rishad will be here for hours. He told me not to wait for him.'

The ground floor Devi had rented for him belonged to a Mrs. Kartik who herself lived in a trim annexe near the gate where she ran a beauty parlour for a select clientele. Yesterday Mrs. Kartik had enquired sympathetically, 'You're all alone?' looking about for a photograph of wife or family among the possessions he had unpacked. Michael supposed he was. Either sympathy for his solitary status or curiosity made her pop up at her window to wave cheerfully as he had left the house to dine at Devi's, and to appear at his doorstep with a bowl of nasturtiums this morning. Tonight she was asleep or at the Gymkhana Club where she had told him she played cards three times a week. He invited Devi in.

Layer upon layer of stifling heat, depth upon depth of darkness assailed them as Michael shut the front door behind them and stood leaning against it. Inside, the temperature had a thick animal presence that for a moment displaced all emotion and action. He imagined ice, frozen buckets of it, and tall glasses of water. He switched on the light. The furnace heat made everything look shabby. The nasturtiums were wizened in their bowl on the telephone table, the multi-colour print of the tablecloth, the colour of an upholstered chair, the curtains hanging exhausted and shapeless at the end of the entrance hall offended his senses. His eyes longed for cool transparence, anything that would not strike and blister the sight. Doubt flooded him about bringing Devi here at this time. Events, private and historic, trespassed on the current of communication that had flowed so easily between them at the party and on the way here.

He remembered he had never been alone with this woman. She had always put a man, her race, her family between them. Everything converged now on the need to settle this once and for all without illusion. He wanted no sudden violent possession after all these years. Some instinct for self-preservation in him needed to know whether she had succumbed to the mythology with which her countrymen surrounded their deepest concerns, or was willing to step out into a reality of her own choice. Their hands touched and her eyes had a look of pain and pleading that told him nothing stood between them any more. In the bedroom they lay holding each other on the bed, fully dressed, afraid to separate. To her surprise Devi began to cry convulsively, her face against his shirt, a breakdown she later thought of as a burst of frantic sorrow for something that had not yet happened, and as if she knew the terrible uselessness of her tears to prevent it. She wiped her eyes with the handkerchief Michael gave her and said, 'It's the last straw when one doesn't know what one's crying about.'

'I'll get us some water,' said Michael, 'I meant to before we came in here.'

It was ice-cold and calming. He had brought some whisky too for himself, and settled himself on the bed beside her again.

'One can influence other people's children – I make speeches all over the country to students and I get some response – it's one's own one can't reach,' said Devi.

'Perhaps it's a vanity to try.'

'It's a duty,' she said, and remembered his crossing swords with her over the word.

She talked, most of the time not expecting answers, out loud to herself, a soliloquy twisted with apprehension, beginning and ending with Rishad. She told him in between about Madhu who had arrived, driven by God knew what desperation, at her house before breakfast yesterday, to beg Devi to prevent her marriage. Her parents had started negotiations with a Delhi family. Madhu, crazed and ill, had crouched in her chair, refusing the anaemic comfort of words. Devi, telling Michael of the girl's tragedy, said wearily that parents could be persuaded to delay almost anything except a girl's marriage. There was a tribal fanaticism about girl-disposal. She talked till at the end of a sentence a total silence descended on them and the night outside. It was an armed truce, not peace, poised for tumult again at daybreak when noise and a quickly unbearable brightness would clash in the street. Through the rare quiet Michael felt the quality of dominant life in Devi that attracted him so much return to her, and he wondered how many men enjoyed a woman so essentially tough and capable. She turned to him and with the insight and extravagance she had always brought to loving made their coming together both simple and epic. She said afterwards, 'I have no ambition left so I must really be in love.' An older love than she admitted, thought Michael, but with nothing preying on it any more.

Rishad lay on his back looking up at the veiled stars. There was the faintest mist and the air had a fraction of a nip at this hour. He could not have borne contact with even a sheet in his room at home, but here in the open he was glad of the blanket folded under him. It was padding between him and the loosely packed granite blocks and stones in the back of the truck. His companion had fallen asleep. They had had to wait an hour at the quarry outside Delhi while the stone-breakers loaded the truck and with its scheduled load placed in it the two boxes of explosives they had kept hidden in their huts, more material for the current phase of the experiment. Naren had said it would take ten years to achieve a successful upheaval. Before he fell ill he had not been discouraged about its progress. He was a skilled organizer and under him they had mounted a flawless campaign. What looked like sporadic violence was carefully programmed beforehand and its effects minutely studied. They were trying to collect data of the official and public reaction to explosions, to the disrupting of water mains and the removal of fish plates from railroad tracks. It was a scientific experiment to see what worked, what didn't, and why. They had been trained for their work. Some of it needed lightning calculation. A hand grenade allowed only seconds between the removal of the pin releasing the lever and the actual explosion. Chiefly they worked at organizing sections of workers. Rashid's group concentrated on the quarry and its environs. It had been going so well till Naren fell ill. Or had Naren's boundless energy and optimism given them the illusion that it was going well? Rishad tried to wipe out the mental image of Naren ill, perhaps dying, without a doctor.

He shifted his position and tried to fall asleep. At the point of losing consciousness he always jolted alertly awake by the lethal possibilities of the boxes he was travelling with. He felt dazed and afloat between darkness and dawn as the lorry lumbered its unmanoeuvrable way to the city, joined by other trucks. Last night's miraculous voice threaded through the road noises, hauntingly beautiful to recall. It had been hard to tear himself away from the singer at Pinky's house. On some nights the road came alive with the roar and grind and thunder of the monster vehicles straddling it. He felt the disturbance around him as part of his own, when he felt he'd never known anything but the road. Yet it was cool and dark and the night's work was nearly done. It would be completed when the explosives were safely delivered to their city destination. There was not the tension of the outward journey, though they lived with fears of being seen, absences from home noticed, a police trail laid to the site where their contacts were and the material of destruction stored. Delhi was surprisingly sanguine because it was the capital, lavish security arrangements surrounding each Minister's house and movements, while the rich had chowkidars to guard them. The huge average population lived outside this concern.

He had first met the quarry workers months ago, yet instead of becoming more human, more individual as exchanges between him and them took on more familiarity, the end of each meeting brought down a curtain between them. He was on one side of the curtain, going home, going toward a future. They were on the other side, rooted in their time-stopped existence. They had the immovability of the quarry, the massive inertness of the poundage and tonnage of rock they mined and broke and lifted in monotonous headloads over monotonous hours to fill each truck that carted them to Delhi for construction. They had that stone-anciency. Rishad's group worked with the casteless, the Untouchables. The newspapers called them 'underprivileged', 'the weaker section'. To Rishad they were scarcely human. They lived from day to day, from hand to mouth, not with the vagabond carelessness of gypsies, but of people with nowhere to go. The outskirts of Delhi or the fringe of society or the edge of history, it was all the same thing. They were people who hadn't known they were people until Rishad and his group under Naren's direction had started teaching them they were, explaining they need not work as many hours as they did, that they were entitled to more pay, that if a marauding caste neighbour set fire to one of their huts or raped one of their women, they need not suffer it. The law provided redress. How difficult just to teach them they were human. The law, of course, said they were, and all their rights were on the statute book. But they couldn't read and those in authority had not taken the trouble to see that the laws were observed, and if they did, justice was slow and layers of sluggish procedure clogged each step of it. The law of the land lay like disintegrated rubble in the quarry. Only Naren seemed able to unearth their humanity. With Naren they talked, gathered around him and complained, squatted and listened. Naren had not come and gone. He had lived with them. His mission to mould them into an organized group had been cut short when he fell ill. They were carrying it on, but it was not the same. And their other activities were getting looser, not so well planned. A dangerous amateurishness had crept into the campaign. Rishad sat up and woke his companion as they entered Delhi. Last night's concert, the magical singer at Pinky's house, vanished like a dream.

10

The hall where the concert was being held was only half full. Even the 'professional musicians' advertised hadn't drawn much of a crowd. A girl selling programmes in the centre aisle saw Rishad hesitate in the doorway and waved frantically.

'Come in, there's plenty of room,' which he could see for himself. Too bad, when all the third-rate movies had crowds fighting to get in from 9 a.m. on.

But he had spent more time than he had planned in the library and now time was short. He looked at his watch.

'Oh, come on,' she wheedled anxiously, 'It's in a good cause. We need all the support we can get. You don't know what it is like to be on the stage and see empty seats in the front rows. It's about to begin.'

He bought a ticket from her and went down a side aisle, slipping into a fourth row seat under a fan, as the curtain went up on a trio of musicians sitting cross-legged on a smooth white sheet. He was only half listening as the music began, until the insistent beat of the tabla demanded his attention. A shining ribbon of sitar melody wound silkily in and out of the tabla beat, captive to it. It broadened into langour, blurred and branched into a lace-like intricacy, vanishing into the beat and reappearing in embroidered rosettes of sound. And now it was a single luminous flow, gliding past the tabla beat, a snake along a petal-strewn path, coming to rest with a fine flourish at a container of cool milk. Rishad startled himself with the simile. His grandmother had once told him snakes loved milk. They were ancient honoured royals. If a snake lifted its hood over a human, as a cobra had once done over his uncle Shivraj's sleeping body, it was a sign of incomparable fortune. One did not kill a snake. One did not kill. Yet Rishad had chosen violence and knew for certain there were times when one must kill. The killing he had not yet done waited for him like a milestone in the distance, a monument some way up the road. He pushed the thought to the back of his mind, but now it overrode the music. From primitive times men had made such a drama of death. Death was death. Why need one feel any awe or exaltation about it or guilt about taking a life? Usman's words the other night had unexpectedly lit up the problem. If you had to kill, you killed without involvement, without personal passion or anger. You did it as a duty. Rishad had never thought particularly about Hinduism fitting the political creed he had made his own. But perhaps it did. Usman's was a queer new slant, or a very old one that hadn't been examined much. Usman had a faculty for pulling out ideas and letting other people make something of them. He enjoyed turning a thousand years of thinking inside out by a single pithy remark, and religion, though not his field, was a favourite subject. Usman had come to the house to talk religion with his grandmother, sitting on the floor of her room beside the chowki where she kept her Ramayana, open at the place where she was reading it, its size and print growing as her eyesight dimmed. For an atheist, Usman was certainly fascinated by religions. His grandmother, all in white, a faint clean scent of cardamom about her, had been the most disciplined person he knew. She had got up every day at first light to have a cold bath and pray. Her religion had made her fast once a week too and feed the neighbourhood poor on that day. It had produced out of the blue a crowd of people he had never seen to carry her bier when she died and walk with it to the cremation place. Rishad clearly remembered her small delicate body draped in a brown shawl and covered with marigolds and a procession that looked like the whole town's poor walking behind it to the river chatting: Ram Nam Satya Hai. None of it made any sense to him, looking back, except the ragged host out of nowhere that had arrived to carry her bier. She so quiet and retiring had had bonds unsuspected with the town's poorest. But bonds like that had to be forged these days without religion.

He hadn't noticed as a child how surrounded they were by the sheer repetition of that name – Ram Nam. Even now, what a lot of Ram's were around. Bhola Ram, Skinny's servant who needed a hearing aid, his mother's P.A., Ram Murti, Ram Ram in greeting, Mansa Ram in the cartoon. If you could tear it out of a single day wherever it cropped up, the day would be full of gaping holes. The durability of myth loomed up like a gigantic obstacle to his task. When he came back to the music the sitar was singing its closing phrases and trailing its last languid ribbon of sound.

The curtain went up next on a cardboard woodland, the set for the Manipuri number. This time the musical accompaniment began to the rhythm of a barrel-shaped drum, slung around the musician's neck. His hands tapped it at both ends, his feet were two birds in the air barely skimming the ground. Krishna, cowherd, lover, god, leaned against a tree. His bamboo flute had a haunting sweetness, irresistibly drawing six dancers toward him from the wings. Rishad sat up and stared. Skinny Jaipal was not just one of the six, she was the main one. He looked hard to make sure she was Radha and she was. A fitted bodice, a stiffly wired short bell-like top skirt of gauze over a brilliant full satin one masked her angularities. Her hair in a classic knot on top of her head had ornaments in it that twinkled and shone through a gossamer veil. Skinny's hands moved with perfect precision, hands that could not so much as hold a coffee cup straight. And all her clumsiness disappeared into this composition of effortless shimmering grace. Rishad was so surprised he felt like laughing out loud. When the lights came on he looked at his programme and saw under Item Two: Radha: Suvarnapriya Jaipal. He got up to go before the third item started, but hung back as the small stooped figure of Dr. P.K. Jaipal passed down the aisle toward the exit. Rishad followed at some distance. Outside the hall Skinny, in face paint and costume, was waiting for her father. She linked her arm with his and walked him to his shabby blue Fiat, chattering animatedly. The troublesome engine whined and stopped and finally started and when it moved off in a flurry of dust she gave it a friendly pat as though it had been a horse. Rishad waited till Skinny came back into the porch and congratulated her on her performance.

'Did you enjoy it? I'm delighted.'

The gracious queen-to-subject act took him aback. Skinny – Suvarnapriya, no less – leaned against a pillar, lipsticked, rouged and mascaraed, the glamour and glitter of her costume putting her beyond ordinary contact. You'd think a year had passed since their last meeting and in the interval she had ascended a throne.

'Music,' she said dreamily, 'I couldn't live without. I've been

studying dance since I was ten.' She adjusted her veil infinitesi-
mally. 'If I were not going on with the study of history, I daresay I
would become a professional dancer.'

Rishad stared, 'Well. Nice seeing you,' he said briefly.

'So nice of you to come,' said Suvarnapriya. She waved her
fingers to him, and went indoors on a swirl of skirts.

Rishad went to his motor-cycle, the oddly sad flute melody in his
head. Single notes piped through slender bamboo produced that
loving lilt. Clouds were piling up and the sky had that queer look of
violent shadows, with something brighter round the edges, that lent
a quality of unbearable suspense to the evening. Suspense was now
natural to him, but the strain sometimes became more than he
could bear. About a mile beyond Daryaganj was the double-storeyed
building of New and Second Hand Books where Naren was hiding
till he could be moved to another place. Controlling his bursting impatience Rishad loitered through the jumbled second hand book collection below and then asked if he could go up and see the rare
manuscripts. He made his way up a flight of steep narrow stairs. He
had been up them so many times he could have climbed them in his
sleep. A sign of danger that, the place had become too familiar and
it was time to move Naren. He was lying on his side on the sagging
niwar bed, facing the wall where monsoon damp had soaked it,
leaving peeling discoloured patches that looked like a scrofulous disease. The room had been swept in the morning but thick sandy dust
had materialized all over it with a kind of hereditary right. In a
corner flies like buzzing black raisins clustered on a remnant of
food. An incense stick stuck into a raw potato on the window ledge
on the side overlooking a back alley failed to keep away mosquitoes
and other insects. Its fume curled upward in a grey thread and in
the early evening the bare room smelled of prayer or death. At
night, the naked bulb suspended on its long wire from the ceiling
gave it another look, of inquisition and a prison cell. From the bathroom the odour of urine battled with disinfectant.

Rishad stood in the doorway, caught in harsh conflicting emotions. All he knew of faith and purpose was centred on the slight
dark-skinned figure motionless on the bed, looking as though he had
not moved since Rishad two weeks ago had undressed and helped
him to lie down, and covered him with fresh linen sheets he had

brought from home. The sheets were stained and crumpled. Rishad had a feeling of utter desolation watching him huddled there. with hardly a sign of life, in a room that seemed part of a huge surrounding stagnation too big to change. It was surely quite different, he thought despairingly, planning change, planning revolution, where stupefying heat was not another character in the action, where there weren't mosquitoes and flies and mildew and vermin, where the whole of nature did not get up and stand in one's way.

Naren turned around in slow motion. He did this by raising himself on his elbows to a nearly sitting position and then lowering himself cautiously on his other side. 'You' was all he said, but each syllable he spoke, because he spoke so few, carried a shocking degree of force. His dark face did not show the fever flush, but his eyes before he closed them again were glazed and veined with fever. It could only be malaria because it came and went, making Naren hot and cold, shivering and helpless and delirious. Rishad sat on the three-legged stool by the bed, his eyes on Naren's face. He knew this face as intimately as he knew the road that had brought him here, and the steep narrowness of the stair. Blind-folded he could have drawn it all on paper. Do you recognize this man, he would be asked one day, if they were unlucky enough. And he would say of course not, for what Rishad recognized was far different from what They wanted – a saboteur, a criminal. That was true, too, depending on which order you served, because it was Naren who had schooled Rishad in the use of small arms, trained him to make the most of their deadly capacity, battles in which the user remained hidden, and the aim was accurate, smokeless and almost soundless. What Rishad saw was the stark beauty of Naren's life, all its meaning inscribed in the livid wounds on his back. They would in any case recognize Naren by his back. They needed no other evidence but the intricate map of burns they had themselves scorched into his flesh. Flesh that had tried to heal and shrivel into scars and scabs, but had failed and given up. Raw rebellious ridges of it rose, with angry pulp in between. With what had they done it, and had Naren's voice, now so hoarse, been rubbed out by his screams? Or had he borne the torture without a cry? Rishad had never asked and Naren had never spoken of it. They would also know him by the skin of his ankles, shackled together to prevent his escape. Yet he had finally escaped.

Naren opened his eyes and said 'Go' but Rishad kept vigil a little longer. It was part of his mental exercise every time he came here to reconstruct that map of wounds. Usually he bathed and dressed them when he cleaned Naren up, but today Naren was too ill for any ministrations. He would not have dismissed Rishad so soon. And these days his 'Go' sounded like defeat, not dismissal. Rishad knew now that the uprising he had worked for was over before it had got going. The movement so promisingly begun had collapsed. It had not been able to create a proper revolutionary centre. Its members were scattered and disorganized. A star had risen, glittered briefly and burnt out. Its leaders like Naren had become hunted fugitives or too broken-bodied to carry on. Its followers waited tensely in darkness for orders that did not come. Some few went on with local isolated programmes of their own. But they had to face it now that without proper leadership these wouldn't add up to anything important. They only kept the thing simmering and morale from fading altogether. Yet Rishad was convinced it needed only one supreme event to revive it. Only one. And every time he came he hoped Naren would be well enough to talk of it.

He got up, nearly forgetting to leave what he had brought, three pills wrapped in a scrap of paper. He took them from his pocket and added them to the small pile in the empty cigarette packet on the battered suitcase under Naren's bed. Skinny got them from her father's dispensary when she could. For a comrade in pain, he had told her. They *were* painkillers and sometimes Naren did take them for pain. But enough of them would give him a way out if he needed it. It was Rishad's compact, his rational arrangement with Naren. Yet each day that Naren lived was a reprieve from the task Rishad had undertaken, to provide certain death as an act of love and service. He stood over the bed, tears in his eyes, wanting to cry out, 'Live! Only *live*, and we will do what we have to do together.' Unbelievable that the end might come here in this room, in this decrepitude and dirt, for what remained of Naren, product of the best school in India, an honours graduate from Harvard, a Ph.D. from Oxford. How simple he had remained in spite of all that, involved with other men's misery, when he could have had the earth and its prizes to do what he liked with.

What a man Naren had been. The past tense with its memory of health and vitality hurt and Rishad jerked away from it. Naren's talk was so incisive, his laughter so irrepressible, that Rishad had lost the taste for any other talk. Conversations with the famous and the glamorous, whom he met in his mother's house, were usually so sterile in comparison. So few of the 'great' had real substance, only reputations built on layers of froth ending in fame and riches and clever talk. They were insipid beside the tumultuous reality of this one man. A man who had chosen the hard life, acquainted himself with the harsh heat and torrential rain of unhealthy places and people who would not remotely have crossed his path in the privileged life he had been born to. It was that magic of communication Rishad had envied Naren most and felt so isolated from himself.

A breeze blew in from the window, drying the sweat on Naren's face and sending a tremor through his body. Rishad adjusted the sheet round him. He walked softly out, down the stairs and lingered among the dusty bookshelves. Familiar titles wavered and shook through his tears. He blew his nose and stepped out into the road. The rim of bright light at the sky's edges had expanded and suffused the sky around it with electric colour, hurting his eyes.

'I don't know what to make of it,' said Michael, taking the gin and lime the bearer brought him on a tray of heavy Georgian silver, 'I never imagined they'd want to vet my manuscript.'

The British High Commissioner's residence remained on the avenue known as St. George's. It had not moved to Chanakyapuri where most missions had built new embassies, and where the chancery and apartments for the High Commission's officers were. The house at the corner of St. George's Avenue was informal and friendly, with only portraits of the Queen and Prince Philip in the hall to show it was official, not private. Michael had been taken into the air-conditioned drawing room. Through the glass doors he had a restful view of well-watered grass and flowerbeds. The sprinklers were going round and round the shady patch of lawn. In the few minutes it had taken the High Commissioner to join him the recollection of the scalding taxi drive here had receded. He felt cool, comfortable, dry.

The High Commissioner said, 'Annoying, isn't it, but they feel they have to be careful.'

'Of *books*?'

'Of outside influences generally. They're very sensitive about them. It's understandable.'

Either you understood that kind of thing or you didn't. Michael didn't. A prickly heat rash on his chest and arms was making him irritable and his second gin and lime was going to his head. Either there was too much gin in it or it was the heat. The High Commissioner had barely touched his first.

Michael said, 'This is something new. When I was here last you could write anything you liked, photograph any slum. Some uncomplimentary stuff got published, but it never did much damage and nobody here bothered about it. Shivraj took the view that any danger to India could only come from its own people, not from outside.'

'You were brought up here,' said Sir Humphrey.

'Only till the age of eight.'

The High Commissioner looked less haggard when he smiled. 'I had the impression you'd lived here as an adult.'

'I did. Much later on.'

'There's no *policy* as such,' said Sir Humphrey, reflecting, 'but there's a general *drift* in the direction of more controls over newspapers, films, books and so on, more censorship, though it isn't defined.'

Michael retorted that there was nothing undefined about the 200-odd pages of manuscript he had so far completed sitting squarely on the table of some major or minor official of the Information Ministry.

Sir Humphrey went on, 'The Prime Minister is absolutely committed to the free circulation of ideas himself. He's said so more than once. One has to try and understand the problems he's up against.'

'I'm trying,' said Michael.

Sir Humphrey had dealt with more boorish guests than Michael. Half his job consisted of being pleasant and civilized in all weathers.

'Wouldn't you think it obnoxious interference if a book being written by a foreigner had to be vetted by some Ministry at home?' demanded Michael.

'Oh my dear fellow,' Sir Humphrey laughed off the idea, 'let's go in to lunch.'

At lunch, laid for two at one end of a polished table, on cobweb mats, with an ornate silver bowl of mangoes and bananas between them, he said, 'Well, you have more knowledge of this country than I have, Mr. Calvert, but it *is* an Asian country.'

'It always was,' said Michael.

'And therefore we can't apply our yardsticks here.'

'It's not our yardstick I'm applying. It's theirs. This censorship racket is new. Intolerance was never part of their tradition.'

'I daresay that was the British connection rubbing off on them. It's worn off. They feel now they've got to contend with all the different strains and pulls in the country and bring them into line if they want to get ahead. They want a more homogeneous outlook.'

'Where on this earth can you find three and a half million square kilometres of territory with a population of over five hundred million, that has a homogeneous outlook – unless it has been bludgeoned into it? Homogeneity was never a value here.'

The High Commissioner courteously pursued his point. 'As I see it, what they're trying to build up – understandably – *is* a reasonable degree of uniformity. When you travel up and down this country you realize how necessary that is. The P.M. is very popular, you know, though a bit authoritarian for some tastes, but that's a Western prejudice again. These people need a strong leader, a father figure. Shivraj was just that.'

'Shivraj was a democrat,' said Michael.

'Indeed he was, indeed he was, but that may have been in part the British inheritance.'

'He never denied what he got from the British,' said Michael, putting his knife and fork down carefully side by side on his empty plate, 'but this is a staggeringly old country. It makes my head spin to think how old it is. Older than the rocks. Old and settled and structured when Britons were painting their bodies blue. Already old when their epics and ancient books before the epics were written. That way of life and thinking still exists, and not only in the village. It's there in the factory and the bazaar. It's there if you scratch the surface of anyone who calls himself a modern Indian.

It's a colossal storehouse, some of it evil and repellent, and some of it as fine as the world has produced and very relevant to modern times, bombs and all. What rubbed off or didn't rub off from the British is really beside the point. They've got five thousand years of tradition to dip into. And nowhere does it come up with intolerance.'

In his mind's eye was a copy of his manuscript on the desk of some bureaucrat who knew nothing of Shivraj's character, or if he did, and approved what he read, might not have the courage to say so, if what this incredible old stick was saying was true. Michael drained his wine glass for the third time and remembered his manners.

'I'm sorry if I've been abrupt.'

'Not at all, don't give it a thought. I can understand your being upset about this business.'

'It's not that books have to be read,' said Michael, 'Nobody has to read a book if he doesn't want to. So why this fuss?'

'The trouble with yours,' said Sir Humphrey, paying him an urbane compliment, 'is that it's likely to be read. And then there's the official biography coming out and I suppose they're keen there shouldn't be anything contradictory.'

'For God's sake, why not? People *are* contradictory. There should be ten different interpretations of Shivraj, instead of what I see will happen – a string of stereotype biographies. I know the man who's doing the official one which will probably be the model for the next six. He didn't know Shivraj from the back of a bus.'

'Oh really'

'When this kind of thing begins to happen, interpretative writing disappears. Second-hand stuff, official handouts take its place. Scholarship becomes a farce. This man incidentally hasn't been to see Shivraj's sister once.'

'She's a charming woman,' said Sir Humphrey.

'She knew Shivraj as few people did.' He added roughly, 'For her the holiest words in the language were "my brother" '.

'Yes, I understand they were close.'

Michael was tempted to laugh hilariously, to send the Spode china rattling with his laughter. He restrained himself with an effort and congratulated himself on his restraint. He had eaten three light excellently cooked courses, drunk a good wine, and taken nearly an hour so far of the old boy's time. For behaviour he would be given two out of ten marks. No need to reduce it to zero. He pictured Sir Humphrey and his aides discussing India starting at twelve minutes to two today. Perhaps it was Michael who was off-key, not they. He should have been a Humphrey Scott or a bright new Englishman on a brand new scene and then the whole complicated clutching past would not have mattered.

'I understand yours isn't a political book,' said Sir Humphrey over coffee in the drawing room, 'This vetting won't amount to anything. It's probably only a formality.'

'Shivraj was the country's undisputed leader for ten years of power, and for many years before that. How can you leave politics out of that?'

Sir Humphrey acknowledged the difficulty. 'Well, I shall be most interested to know what they say. In any case it won't affect publication elsewhere.'

'No,' said Michael dryly.

'And of course if there's anything I can do, I shall be glad to.'

Michael got up. 'You've been very kind.'

His taxi drove up Janpath where he had an impulse to get down at the row of shops selling Tibetan ware. He walked up and down looking. Devi was attracted to Tibetan art and craft. Now, at half-past two, the sun was at its most devilish with a leering ferocity about it. Michael's hair felt like damp straw, his skin felt scarlet. He went into Shop Number Twelve. The rosy-cheeked, broad-faced woman, with a neat plait wound round her sleek head, kept her hands folded tranquilly on the striped apron of her dark long-sleeved dress, looking as if she had never stepped down from the world's highest plateau, while he picked up loose stones of jade, amber and amethyst, or their imitations, and let them run through his fingers, and turned carved boxes of silver inlaid with onyx or turquoise around in his hands. His attention was caught by a pendant that belonged to another class of workmanship altogether, a large smoky topaz in an old-fashioned silver setting, on a cheap tin chain.

'How much' he asked.

'One hundred and fifty rupees.'

'Like hell it is.'

'It is real' she said goodnaturedly.

He could see it was, and that at Harrods it would have cost at least ten times that figure, its setting classed as 'antique.'

'Take it for your lady,' she suggested.

'Unfortunately my lady does not wear jewels.'

Her slanting black eyes showed what she thought of ladies who didn't.

'But I'll take it anyway, without that tin chain.'

She snipped off the chain and wrapped the pendant in tissue paper. He put it in his pocket. He walked a few yards to the left and through the gates of the Imperial Hotel. The drive was deserted. A few cars were parked in a strip of shade on the far side. The young man at the tourist agency counter in the lobby said cheerfully, 'Hello, Mr. Calvert. "Mad dogs and Englishmen" – you look hot.'

'I am. Can you lead me to a glacier? I came in to cool off.'

He walked into the espresso bar and ordered a large lemon squash from the solitary attendant. There was not another soul in sight and the terrace outside sent up messages of white fiery heat. Its cane furniture had been stacked in a corner until later, when it would be set out under garden umbrellas again. No one wandered around at this hour who didn't have to. Michael was disturbed. He had become afflicted with the Devi disease, the Usman disease, with their unspoken unhappiness that God was not in his heaven and all was not right with their world. Now he believed it and understood its emotional and spiritual impact on these friends of his as if he had passed through an invisible barrier and stood on their side of it. Shivraj had said the age of nationalism would be over once freedom was achieved, that every man should belong in several worlds, as many as he cared to. Yet frontiers were closing, shutters of the mind coming down here as in the rest of Asia. Nationalism must be a disease there was no getting rid of. Shivraj had not reckoned with its hold. Shivraj had been wrong. And Shivraj, said Michael to himself, is dead. He had not believed it even on the day in London when he had read the news and mourned his physical passing, and certainly not as he breathed life into Shivraj's personality day by day through the pages of his book. Yet now, here in his country, he knew Shivraj was dead, for there is no one more dead than the ignored and forgotten. He finished his lemon squash, took a taxi home and fell into a deep drugged sleep, waking unrefreshed. At six o'clock Devi arrived unannounced.

Their time together was so rationed that each meeting seemed large and leisurely. In one hour you could, for example, sip an iced drink, talk and listen with the same keen appetite you afterwards gave to making love, with no feeling of hurry through any of it, and today he felt he had new points of contact with her and understood her queer isolation.

'How did your work go today' she asked.

'It didn't go.' He told her about his book and that he had felt too irritated to work after handing it to the Ministry. Devi, who took a proprietary interest in the manuscript, which he was certain she would not have if it had been about Suleiman the Magnificent or some other worthy or colourful character, said with severity, 'I still have some influence – I think. I can speak to the Information Minister.' And then she added, 'But I won't.'

'No,' he agreed, 'but it's damnable and I felt like smashing every bit of Spode china in the embassy. I was a social disaster.' He remembered the topaz pendant and brought it to her. 'It has been a strange unhappy day. I've discovered Shivraj is dead.'

She looked up from the topaz and what she was going to say about it died on her lips. Instinctively seeking shelter, she moved closer to Michael, sat within his shielding embrace. And the epochal sadness of Shivraj's death, and what had died with him, held them both.

Devi was living a perfectly normal life – normal, that is, to people who ran countries. It consisted at times of taking decisions where mistakes could lead to disaster, and its issues revolved around some point outside and far from oneself. The day once begun, never officially ended. It merely changed its official pace and content and went on. The steady stream of early morning callers at the house acquired a more sophisticated level in the office with political and formal interviews, people to discuss their cases and contracts. She had not arrived in office until noon today because she had had to be in Parliament during question hour. Yet in the eight hours she had sat here – the realization staggered her – she had scarcely put pen to paper. Shivraj had been right. One could forget to read and write in this job. The Secretary to the Ministry did all the writing, composing his own verbiage from the line she laid down. And her Secretary was the only person in her official environment from whom, try as she might, she had not been able to get a frank and easy response. A pallid-looking man more than midway through his service, the new government's call for committed civil servants seemed to have flung him into a civil servant's nightmare, a kind of agony of constipation, so that now he looked uncertain even when to smile. The only time he had dined at her house he had been so eclipsed by his socially overpowering wife that in pity she had never asked him again. Maybe it was his wife and not administration under new political masters that accounted for his pallor. That, and not being able to respond to anything she suggested till he knew which way the Secretariat wind blew.

One could forget there *was* life outside this office. There was no such thing as a weekend or even a Sunday undisturbed and the chain of unconnected cases and personalities that paraded through her day left her quite flattened. It gave her no time to think a problem through. This evening she wanted to go through Usman's paper without being interrupted. She needed isolation to do it justice. No one else had ever made her feel uneducated. She and Shivraj had been immersed in the demands of the national movement. It had been their life. But for Usman, *life*, the singing voice, was another thing altogether.

Devi had sent the members of her staff home and had told Ajaib Singh she would not need him till after ten. She had cleared her glass-topped table of files and impediments, as though the extra space might aid calm reflection. From under her desk, at one end of the rectangular room, blue and beige carpet extended to the opposite wall, a pleasant expanse that showed since she had moved the sofa and chairs and oval table to the far end of the room near the window. The striped curtains, no matter how they were altered or adjusted, ended up hanging crooked. Their dipping and sagging had distracted her at first. Now it was an unimportant detail. She had come to the regretful conclusion that nothing around her would be perfect unless she went crazy trying to perfect it. She had learned (with Ram Murti's help) to understand her priorities. There was no sign of another presence in the building and that was typical of her life too. She was either surrounded by people she hardly knew or entirely alone – a reminder that the people she had done her real living and dying with were gone.

She had finished making notes on Usman's document an hour later when she heard a light tap on the door and looked up to find him standing in the half-open doorway, recognizing him in the shadowed room half-intuitively even before she saw his arm-sling. What a long time his arm was taking to mend. He had a parcel in one hand. Usman's first thought, seeing her lost in concentration at her desk, was that her desk too had become a barricade. Somewhere behind it meaning was getting lost. Will we all have to come out from behind our desks then, he wondered, and knew that for him and Devi, if he understood her correctly, the time had come.

'I went to your house, Shahbano, and they told me you were still here.'

'I'm sorry, Usman,' said Devi tiredly, 'Were we supposed to meet this evening?'

'We had a tentative appointment. Nothing that Ram Murti had written down,' he added with a twinkle, 'Kirti told me you hadn't eaten so I brought you some dinner.'

He sat down opposite her and unwrapped muslin-thin rotis, hot seekh kababs and as a concession to her, some vegetable in its earthen container. The ceremony, accomplished with one hand, took time and Devi sat watching it, a pleasant anticipation beginning to steal over her. Usman, oddly, did not drink, despite everything else about him belonging to a wine culture. The arts and pursuits of leisure, the sense of style that pervaded all his actions, distinguished him from everyone else she knew.

'I'm starved,' she said eagerly, 'I didn't know I was.'

'A very revealing statement,' he said, with an answering smile, wrapping a kabab in roti and passing it to her across her desk.

She ate with pleasure. Refreshed and cheerful with food inside her she poured iced water for both of them from the flask near her desk.

'I've been going through your paper again,' she said.

She touched the document as she spoke. Usman had, with infinite care, taken the prevailing educational pattern apart and in prose approaching literature had put it together again. He had suggested outlets for skill and training before university age and drilled neat holes in current theories about higher education being everyone's inalienable right. He had recommended an end to the weed-burst of new universities and the free functioning of those that existed. None of this was original. A commission appointed by Shivraj had made more or less the same recommendations, only they were more urgent now. Usman's own contribution was an outline of a new pattern that stood education down squarely in its own cultural milieu and envisaged experiments where it became a two-way process between the teacher and the taught. He had also attached a three-page appendix on housing. He listened while Devi went over these points, looking, he thought, as animated as if her day had just begun.

He said when she had finished, 'What chance do you think it has of acceptance?'

She had not been prepared for the question.

'You do see the flaw in it, don't you, Shahbano?'

'What flaw?' she asked.

'That if we go to it with a will it is likely to work.'

'I don't follow you.'

'No, you wouldn't. You belong to too practical a breed. To you it sounds quite possible and sensible even though it will upset the present system. The trouble is, it doesn't fit in with the book of rules we're up against. The burning concern for the masses doesn't burn quite as the book says. This whole document could relieve me of my post. In any case, that is what I came to talk about. I want to resign.'

Devi said nothing. She could not allow Usman's resignation. What good would it do? and she would lose an irreplaceable ally.

'I'm not very effective where I am, you know,' he said.

Earlier in the day she had been shown a list of new academic appointments to the university. Two names proposed by Usman had not been on it. And the list had been drawn up without consultation with her. Apparently she was not very effective either.

'Take the matter of professors or students involved in acts of violence – ' he went on.

'What happened about the three who raped the girl?' she interrupted.

'They've been found and I've been directed to take them back.'

Devi examined her nails. The foreign press had called Shivraj's silences taciturn. They had labelled him with destructive little one and two-word flourishes that could smear an image for millions of readers. But at times such as this what on earth was there to do but keep silent?

'You can't make a revolution in thin air,' said Usman, 'It has to come from the ground under your feet, your own ground. And that's what I really came to see you about.'

She looked up, affection and amusement in her eyes, but asked warily, 'About revolution?'

Usman leaned forward. 'I see something taking shape and it has the face of chaos. We've got to avert that. I think I can if I can take the students with me. I've already discussed it with some of them and with a number of faculty members. We can make Delhi the laboratory of this experiment. If your Cabinet turns it down I'm going to campaign for it in the streets with the students.'

'Don't', said Devi sharply, 'there's enough going on in the streets.'

'Of the wrong kind,' said Usman, 'If the educated don't take to the streets now, in the proper way, the mob will.'

'The proper way?' Devi felt the discussion had slipped from her, gone further than she could follow. She was suddenly afraid.

Usman sat back and explained. He had always been persuasive. But this was even more than an argument. It was a cause, a choice to be made without delay, and the way of action would be non-violence.

'The "Hindu" way you were talking about the other night,' she said, faintly mocking.

'The only way, Shahbano. The State owns the big guns. Any confrontation with it, if it's to succeed, must be non-violent. There never was another way. Besides, do you realize it's the only way most people in this country understand and will give their allegiance to?'

If he had expected another spirited rebuttal from Devi, he did not get it. She looked up from the document on which he had laboured, and said, 'I'll join you.'

Usman laughed. He sounded exultant. He reached with his good arm across the desk and covered both her hands with his. 'That's why I love you. I love you more than I can say.'

She nodded, tears springing to her eyes. 'When is that silly arm of yours going to be all right? Does it take so long for fractures to mend? Or are you going to go around in a sling for the rest of your life?'

But he was talking about his plans. She was aware of Usman's intensities. Each one led him into action in a blaze of singlemindedness and when this stage was reached in his thinking, there was no stopping him. She also knew he was no visionary but a meticulous planner assisted by sensitive antennae of his own. She trusted both his judgment and his instincts. But had it come to this all over again? She tried to picture it and it was easy enough because she had spent years of her life in mass meetings and demonstrations. She knew protest and where it led. Confrontation was never pretty. Once it had been multitudes with the surge of an ocean and the fire of righteousness about them demanding something inalienably theirs – freedom. This, from the crying need for educational reform, could fan out into the waiting consciousness and become exactly what Usman had termed it, a revolution from the ground, a hunger and thirst for justice in all its forms. It only needed leadership, and a comparatively unknown Indian, distinguished in academic circles but not a name many outside them knew, had decided to provide it. Foolhardiness could not go much further than the person of this clear-eyed man of nearly fifty with his exacting intellectual and moral standards and his austere insistence on them in his dealings with others. Nor could inspiration.

'What are you thinking of Shahbano?'

'I think you're mad.'

'How interesting. You wouldn't have said that if Shivraj had announced to you one day, "I'm going to take to the streets and I'm certain the people will come with me because it's for a just cause." '

'That would have been different.'

'Oh, would it? You're smitten and hung with charisma like all the rest. We live in a fog, breathing charisma until it chokes us.'

'You're the one who said we are nostalgic for kings – ' said Devi.

'Or some great example that stands out,' finished Usman, 'only what I meant was good example. And that can come from my native village or Shivraj's pedigree. Let's give my village a try.'

Maybe they were making too much of this. The Cabinet might approve Usman's document. All this street business might never happen. If it did, it might not lead to a bigger upheaval. It was all conjecture at the moment. But Usman in his chair across from her looked less in the realm of conjecture than any man she had ever seen. Was it time for unheaval again then? She felt weary at the thought. In this country we never arrive at a resting place. Nothing settles down. Now nothing may for years.

'Talking about taking people with you, what about Nadira?' she asked.

'Have you noticed, those who give themselves with fervour to causes never have anything much to give those nearest them?' He made no attempt to hide his bitterness.

'Except Shivraj,' said Devi.

'Except Shivraj,' he admitted, 'But not me or you. And Michael is another selfish brute. Basically we're all wrapped up in the thing we have to do, as much in the abstract as what's around us. We affect people further out, people we never see, not those near us. Are you in love with Michael?'

Usman had the strong desire as he said it to walk around the desk, hold her against him with his uninjured arm and prevent her lovely mouth from saying anything at all. Devi opened the lowest drawer of her desk and took out her handbag. She picked up her briefcase from where it stood leaning against her chair and put Usman's document into it. She asked, 'Is Rishad one of the students you talked to?'

'I invited him. He didn't come.'

Still, the prospect kindled hope in her. It would give Rishad an opportunity to protest in the open, not through some frightening underground adventure.

She said, 'We'll all wrapped up in the same thing in a sense, you, me and Michael. Of course, I love him. And it's too late now for any of us to be free of the others.'

Hours later a motionless moon yellow with age shining on her face or a confused dream about what Usman was going to do woke her. She sat up in bed with a sense of shock. Sometime earlier it had rained and stopped and the garden still smelled of it. Devi got out of bed and went out onto the lawn. It was fresh and damp under her slippered feet. In the moonlight a figure walked up the path from the gate. She knew instantly it was Rishad returning from an accustomed nocturnal outing and he would not want to be seen. She sat on the moon-drenched verandah, a large part of her understood world falling around her. We who hung out our intentions like flags of rejoicing and gave proud notice to authority when we were going to break unjust laws, have children who come and go clandestinely in the night. She got up, her dread urging her to face this at once. Rishad was slumped in a chair in his room in a posture of utter exhaustion, shadows dark as bruises under his eyes. He did not show any surprise at her entry. There was no trace of defiance or appeal as he looked up at her. Some deep clinging misery about him kept her standing where she was.

He cleared his throat but his voice still came out huskily. 'You're up late. Or is it early?'

Devi said, 'Can you tell me what is wrong?'

He shook his head and cleared his throat again. 'It's nothing personal,' he said inadequately.

'I know.'

He said, 'Let's leave it till morning.'

'Go to bed quickly then.'. She kissed a feverishly warm cheek.

In the morning he had high fever. His recovery days later left him pale and uncommunicative.

The girl stumbled on the threshhold, her slipper catching on the raised lintel. She swooped down to free it, and straightened, drawing the end of her bright cotton sari around her shoulders. Devi saw a young light presence, a face transparent with anxiety and excitement, looking like a woodland creature at the sound of a gun. Behind her Ajaib Singh with the air of having delivered a fairly unimportant document, touched a superior hand to his turban and moved away.

'Come in, Suvarnapriya. I'm happy to meet you,' said Devi.

Seated bolt upright in a straight-backed chair facing her, the girl resembled a fine line drawing, from her narrow-templed face with its elongated narrow eyes and brows to her wrists and hands and feet, and the entire fragile length of her. And much too young to be at university. She took the cup of tea Devi poured for her with an awkwardness that set the cup and saucer rattling. Devi reached out to steady it. Suvarnapriya put it carefully down, cleared her throat, took a deep breath and said rapidly, 'It was very kind of you to send your car for me.' She swallowed, and sat transfixed looking at Devi — Devi, who hadn't even *asked* her if she needed transport, who had just sent it, with a magnificent looking chauffeur and all.

'My dear child, sit more comfortably and drink your tea. And have a piece of cake. It's home-made.'

'You are not at all like Rishad,' said her guest in confusion.

'Really ? What is Rishad like ?'

'Lofty,' Suvarnapriya's eyes scanned the ceiling and swept the room, parodying splendour, 'and grand.'

Before she could decide she had offended her hostess, Rishad's mother laughed delightedly.

'Yes, I suppose he is,' Devi said.

'My father says I talk too much,' the girl said meekly, and in the same breath, 'What a room and a cake.'

Bubbling to the brim, with more words to every sentence than it could hold. A girl to whom anything, anything at all might happen in the years to come. Ships might be launched, cities sacked, rhapsodies sung at a lift of her eyebrow, and yet she was so thoroughly normal and natural her presence here helped to quiet Devi's worries about Rishad's activities. In that moment of silence the girl seemed invisibly to stretch and relax and fill out with ease. Devi glanced around her own drawing room noticing with mild approval that it *was* rather charming and friendly, and had apparently fallen into being that way. Suvarnapriya enthusiastically accepted another piece of cake.

Devi, asking about her father, remembered his name, Jaipal, and it rang a bell. Usman's doctor, whose house had been broken into and one room viciously wrecked. A widower, Usman had told her, living alone with this child. Her alarm was mixed with shame that her every move received police protection while the vulnerable ones went without.

'You know, I forgot to ask Rishad what it is you do, sing or dance. Not that it matters. I need both singers and dancers for my project.'

'I do both.'

'That's very talented of you,' Devi said warmly, 'I wanted to learn dancing as a young girl, but it wasn't considered "nice". What a lot we missed. And I never could sing a note.'

Suvarnapriya's eyes gleamed her amusement and disbelief.

'How's that possible? Rishad likes music.'

'That's from his father, who was musical. And you, do you spend much time on it?'

'As much as I can – what lovely-smelling tea – but that's not much because I'm working for a scholarship so that I can go abroad for post-graduate studies. I love history, too.'

This narrowly-wrought creature seemed altogether too delicate a vehicle to contain so many enthusiasms.

'How is it taught at the university?' asked Devi.

Suvarnapriya made a face. 'Mrs. Gupta reads out notes. We copy.'

Devi thought back to her own schooldays: 'ancient' and 'medieval' times dispensed with, came the trumpets and drums of the British arrival, with its interminable procession of Viceroys and their doings. It had been rewritten in perspective, but evidently rewriting had not made much difference to the teaching. Or maybe Mrs. Gupta was weary with coping and needed time to renew herself. There wasn't one problem, there were ten in each facet Devi glimpsed of the university. The miracle was that an interest in history, and in so much else, could still be born and grow. She was beginning to believe that the survival of the fittest meant the absolute refusal, come what may, of civilized instincts to die.

'Let me tell you about my project,' said Devi.

She described the playlet a young writer of her acquaintance had written. A poet she had commissioned was writing the songs and it was to be enacted for a settlement of villages fifteen miles outside Delhi. The girl listened attentively, breaking in with suggestions enlivened by her gestures.

'But you haven't seen me perform,' she stopped short.

'Will one day next week suit you for a rehearsal? We'll need another girl and two young men. Will you be able to enlist them?'

Suvarnapriya nodded. She was a dancer all right. Each look and gesture spoke volumes. Devi heard footsteps in the corridor and was glad Rishad had returned. It was Michael.

'Come and join us, Michael,' She introduced them to each other.

'You write biographies,' Suvarnapriya informed him.

'The girl reads,' Michael rejoiced, taking a cup of tea from Devi.

'And sings and dances,' said Devi, explaining the purpose of her visit.

'If I weren't stuck with another book I'd beg to be taken along,' he said.

Suvarnapriya's face reflected the glow and flicker of rapid impressions, too many to take in at one time.

'By the way, what does Rishad call you?' Devi asked, 'or do you always go by your whole name?'

'Rishad calls me you. My father and my friends call me Priya.'

In the middle of a story about her father, Suvarnapriya remembered she was in a Minister's house and couldn't settle down for an evening's cosy chat. Reluctantly she got up to go. Devi was saying, 'I *am* sorry Rishad wasn't here', when he walked in. He stood surveying his mother's guest blankly for a minute before he said hello. Suvarnapriya gave Devi an eloquent look out of her long narrow eyes, then said goodbye and thank you, and Devi replied twinkling, 'The car is waiting to take you home.'

Rishad said, 'Don't bother, Mum, I'll take her back. I have to go that way. In fact I'd forgotten she was coming or I'd have told you earlier. Hello Michael.'

Devi and Michael went to the front door to see them off.

'What in heaven's name is the child doing?' Michael demanded.

'Tucking her sari up,' said Devi.

Suvarnapriya had also taken the loose end of her sari and wrapped it round her head and throat.

'She might be taking off for the moon. Wonder why she didn't go in the car?'

'It's not often you get a lift from the lofty,' said Devi, 'and when you do, you take it if it kills you.'

Outside Rishad was regretting having offered Skinny a lift. He remembered too late the paraphernalia of persuasion and preparation that had surrounded his previous offer. The girl was crazy.

'Now hang on to me or you'll fall off,' he ordered, starting the engine.

'It's quite all right,' she said, nervously watching the two people in the doorway.

'Don't be moronic. Do you want to fall off?'

Suvarnapriya extended her thin arms and clasped them cautiously around his middle. The appalling nerve of me, she thought astounded at her boldness, tearing down a public thoroughfare clutching a man. Clutching of all people, *this* man whom everybody knew, with his famous fascinating mother and his record-breaking marks. And it was getting to be a habit. The first time at least no one she knew had seen her. She fervently hoped her father and Bhola Ram would not be at home to see them arrive. Papa could be explained to but Bhola Ram would have a fit. The motor-cycle swung around a corner and she tightened her arms around him. Her cheek against his back, she had a peculiar drowning sensation. She closed her eyes and moved her face so that her lips were pressed against his shirt.

'That's right, hold tight,' Rishad yelled above the roar.

Thank God no one was around as they sputtered in. She asked Rishad to come in for a cool drink, provided there were lemons in the

123

house. Sometimes Bhola Ram forgot to bring them, or remembered and didn't because the price had gone up. But Rishad said he wouldn't come in. He noticed the ride had given her a funny glazed look. He wiped his face with his handkerchief and ballooned his shirt out to let some breeze through. The house gave him a twinge. He felt about it as he had once years ago about eating a chicken he'd played with before he saw Kirti wringing its neck in the back yard. He hadn't wanted to eat a chicken he had memories of and it bothered him to accept Skinny's hospitality in a house he had raided. But there was more than half an hour to kill before he met his companions at the Red Fort and he might as well spend it cooling off.

Skinny took him through the living room, shabby with old wicker furniture. Rishad was not given to imagining but he guessed there'd probably be a worn carpet on the floor in winter. With or without it the room had the stamp of actual poverty. How could he ever have mistaken it for one of affluence, except that it was in a good middle-class neighbourhood or had once been. But incomes didn't buy what they once had and many people's life style may have slid downward unobserved by people like him. Compared with the really poor, this street would be well off, but how 'rich' was it, in fact? On a table there was a picture of a stern young bridal couple, Skinny's parents, staring straight into the camera as if they knew the care-free years were over and the life of the householder begun, with work to be done, children borne, a living earned. Skinny had gone into the kitchen to make 'nimboo-pani' if there were nimboos, leaving him looking at it.

A living to be earned, Rishad's mind repeated. A distraught man appeared at the door to ask agitatedly if the doctor sahib was in, and rushed away when Rishad shook his head. The steamy warmth of the room folded oppressively around him. Its starkness held the aches and sorrows of one man's life, years of earning a living vanished with nothing to show for it. Nothing but a room so threadbare that even the bruises of time had not left a mark. Yet you knew they were there somewhere, sunk into the walls and floors and beams, sunk and dissolved as they had seemed in the doctor's shrivelled stooped body. Skinny's father should not be waiting for a better life. He should seize it. Then why didn't he, and all the others like him?

Skinny came back with two glasses of 'nimboo-pani' and took him outside the living room where the grass grew raggedly to the verandah's edge. She sniffed and gazed reflectively about her as if she were beside the fountains of the Shalimar and said, 'Don't you love the monsoon? I do.' It jolted Rishad out of his reverie into anger. It was time for her to start hating.

'Keep swirling it around because the sugar settles,' she instructed, swirling the liquid in her own glass, 'Or do you prefer salt and pepper? I never thought of asking you. Isn't that just like me, and with sugar so expensive too. Your mother is terrific.'

Rishad was familiar with the reaction. His mother collected a following without stirring hand or foot. Unreasonably it annoyed him.

'Papa told me how once during the national movement the police locked her up with a bunch of other women they'd arrested. They didn't know who she was and they jeered and poked fun at all the women even when they had to be marched to the toilet outside. Papa was sent for because some of them had been hurt by lathi blows. He said your mother took them all under her wing and kept them in fighting spirits. And when the magistrate wanted to move her to another jail she refused to go. I know lots of stories about your mother.'

Rishad plucked at the long grass, struggling with the thought that others in their time had fought against wrong. But if that had been the right kind of struggle, he said, why were there still so many wrongs?

'You mean we will have perfection?' Skinny asked.

He glanced up suspicious, but Skinny's candid eyes showed no sarcasm.

'No other system has the answers,' he told her, 'It's a world trend now. There's no other way out of economic messes. Every other system is doomed.'

Skinny stirred her drink and licked her finger appreciatively. 'But doom can take a long time to happen.'

The meeting with his mother had affected Skinny oddly. 'What do you mean?' he demanded.

'The Roman empire was doomed but it took about five hundred years to collapse. Five hundred years is quite a long time. Same with the Moghuls. Look how long they took getting to their doom.'

Rishad was exasperated by her slowness to grasp essentials today.

'Nevertheless,' he said emphatically, 'they *were* doomed and they *did* collapse, as obviously those systems had to.'

'Oh naturally, but lots happened before they collapsed. Kathak and ghazals and divine cooking. Painting and poetry and memoirs. And beautiful illuminated manuscripts and the Taj Mahal. Those things never did get doomed. We've still got them, whatever system they came out of.'

The smell of frying onions came from the kitchen. The root-vegetable must be back from wherever he'd been. Rishad got up to go. He felt freer from tension once he'd left her house and was on the road again. The freest life of all would be to belong to no place and be related to no one in friendship or intimacy beyond a point. Knots of tension began with contact. Skinny's house had taken on a woeful accusing personality, its bareness shrieking at him, making him feel rotten about ransacking it. It was like digging up a grave for bones. How different Skinny had looked this evening. Just for a second when he entered his mother's drawing room he hadn't recognized her. Exactly what the difference was he couldn't tell.

It began to drizzle softly. By the time he arrived at the Red Fort it was pouring. The others waited outside and in this downpour there was no use going in. They tried standing under a tree down the road, but the wind rammed the rain at them in chilly gusts and its noise made conversation impossible. Rishad loathed cutting a class but he would have to next morning as it was the only time that suited all of them. They would have to plan their next step carefully. He didn't agree with them about it and was uneasy. The only way to succeed, they had argued, with a leader too ill to lead, was by continuing their campaign of terror. They wanted to keep at it, spread it thin. But Rishad knew from the way their recent performances had gone that there was nothing worse than aimless terror, aimlessly released. Naren had been mathematical about calculating violence and its effects. Without him the groups were fading out or bungling what they did.

He got home soaked to the skin. His mother was sitting turned toward Michael on the sofa in the drawing room, the tea tray still on the table in front of them. She was using her hands to express herself as she did when she got engrossed in a conversation. A tall copper vase filled with glossy leaves glinted in the fireplace. A lavishly embroidered Chinese satin scroll hung above it. Flowers and silk cushions made vivid points of colour in the white-walled high-ceilinged room. The stone floor looked cool and bare between scattered dragon-embossed turquoise and white Tibetan rugs. Here was order and calm, everything in its place, life assembled and arranged with taste and intelligence. His mother looked up.

'Darling Rishi, what a state you're in. You'll be down with fever again. Go and change.'

He came in, leaving a muddy track on the floor and threw himself down on the floor near her. He hadn't, since he was a child, sat like this with his head against her knee. She stroked his wet cheek and hair. Rishad took her hand and sniffed it. He loved the smell of her skin.

'Did you get Helen of Troy home safely?' asked Michael.

'Helen of Troy?'

'Or whatever the Indian version is,' said Michael, 'or maybe she's more like an Etruscan princess.'

'There's no Indian version,' said Devi, 'she's the first of her kind. Unique.'

'Are you talking about —'

'Who else?' said Michael, 'We didn't know such exotica bloomed among your acquaintances.'

Rishad looked from one to the other in bewilderment.

'You see what I mean about him,' said his mother to Michael.

For a few minutes while he drank the cup of tea his mother gave him and heard them talking with quiet amusement and indulgence about him above his head, Rishad knew what contentment and long relationships must be like, and experienced the gentle pace and rhythm his own life lacked. His mind strained into the future, trying to imagine these things for himself, but he couldn't see them.

13

In the middle of September the Cabinet discussed Usman's document the way the Cabinet discussed most things these days, with Minerals and Metals having most of the say. The P.M. didn't say a word. He never did. Sometimes during a Cabinet meeting he said not more than five well-spaced words of one syllable each. Opinion was fairly evenly divided in the Secretariat as to whether he was not very bright, or was, and preferred to keep his own counsel while he listened to other opinions. He was certainly listening to the speaker. Minerals and Metals was the shiniest-eyed radical in the Cabinet and a great favourite. Devi should have known him well. He had followed Shivraj around worshipfully and had been a constant presence at the Party's political committee meetings, strolling in univited, staying because Shivraj, always drawn to the young, had let him. He would arrive at breakfast with a flower – one – for the slim glass cylinder on Shivraj's office table. He would walk along with Shivraj into his dressing room after breakfast to finish discussing a point. He had schemes and his enthusiasm made them attractive. Even his rather hackneyed vocabulary had a charm because it issued from earnestness and youthful confidence. Devi found it had much less charm now. He was saying he was disturbed to find Usman's report ignored 'socio-economic implications' and did not give enough weight to the 'principle of social justice' that higher education should be widely based.

Devi looked up and down the table while he was talking, her brain mechanically registering phrases as they rolled out laboratory-perfect now with repetition. This talk was being echoed, she had no doubt, from the Equator to the Arctic and sideways, wherever like theoreticians foregathered. A pity then that it didn't make more sense. She occupied herself by trying to recall the academic backgrounds of the seventeen at the Cabinet table. M. and M., like the Prime Minister, was a product of the London School of Economics, where both had been considered bright boys. Two of the others had ambled along comfortably at Oxford, one getting a third, but he was making the grade as a politician because he was forthrightly radical. The rest had gone to university here, only one with any distinction. The others had never committed the socio-economic error of drifting so far from the mass as to distinguish themselves in any subject. But they could all talk. And their hearts were in the right place. They were for the Poor and the Small against the Rich and the Big and as proud of it as if they had discovered social justice all by themselves. All they lacked was one good sound sensible programme to put before the country.

She glanced at the youngish faces of this generally well-dressed well-groomed, well-heeled Cabinet and compared it with Shivraj's Cabinet colleagues who had been older, untidier, worn Indian clothes, and, it now struck her, had been each an individual. Impressive personalities, some of them, sticking out like sore thumbs over disagreements on policy, cantankerous at times as if they had toothache, and thoroughly familiar with their subjects and all the prickly practical problems connected with them. Each had made some peculiarly personal contribution, which was what he had been invited to join the Cabinet for. They had been representatives of the intelligentsia themselves but like Shivraj they had been identified in work and sympathy with too many kinds and classes of Indians to want to cut down hefty slices of any of them. There'd been no sheep and goats in Shivraj's time.

Minerals and Metals continued to talk and the others were looking at him the way television showed American Presidents' wives looking at their husbands – faces lit with dazed rapture. Devi became certain his criticism had Cabinet authority and that she was under cross-examination. There was a solid wall, a united will against her. She felt queerly isolated. The Party, the great sheltering Party under whose tutelage she had grown, was now an entity outside her. Only once, long ago, when she had been angry and dismayed at not getting an assignment she had dearly wanted, had she given Shivraj serious offence by speaking disparagingly of the Party. They had been alone together, his voice freezing when he replied, 'This Party led the country to freedom. It made you what you are. If you don't feel privileged to belong to it, you are free to leave it.'

She had been aghast and confused. Leave it and go where, away from the purpose and close comradeship that had been her life? She thought of herself as a creature made and moulded by the opportunities the Party had given her. If she were to go away from it . . . walk away now from these fifteen men and two women who, apart from herself, represented the party leadership in Parliament . . . would anything very calamitous happen? To her surprise she digested the unthinkable thought calmly. It did not shatter her. She turned it over again in her mind. 'A good proposition is like good crystal, Shahbano. The more you hold it up to the light, the better it looks.' That was Usman. The Party all her adult life had meant Shivraj, and she had known what Shivraj stood for. What did it stand for now? Outside the cool controlled capsule of the Cabinet room lay the country, more millions within these frontiers than almost anywhere else on earth. She did not belong with this new aristocracy, these new privileged around the Cabinet table. Usman, one step ahead as usual, had known it before her. But her training and discipline were strong and this was no way to leave. She had not, till this second, ever imagined leaving.

'Sir,' she said to the Prime Minister when M. and M. stopped talking and the other faces could relax into their natural expressions, 'I do implore, before anything further is said that may prejudice the minds of individuals members that we all take time to study this document more carefully.'

Wrong thing, implying M. and M. was prejudiced, also that the others had minds. She could see she had made an enemy of him. He had never regarded her as the right political shade. Perhaps also as that beastly thing, an intractable woman, and definitely as the remnant of a myth. Her going would be correct, for them and for herself, and she did not know why in spite of all this, she wanted to put her face down on her arms and weep.

'Well, now,' said the Prime Minister, a long sentence for him, whatever it meant. He then looked pointedly down the table seeking support. In the bubble of conversation that followed, Devi assumed he had got it and wondered where that left Usman's document. In limbo probably.

Going down the stairs with him after the meeting she wished the P.M. were not so much like the Delphic Oracle, coming out with his enigmatic monosyllables. So different from him at public meetings, where he flayed the Pharisees, as it were, with long curling whip-lashes of emotion, and divided the sheep and the goats with spectac-ular abandon. Get him within four walls and he didn't utter. It was a bit thick to have to spend precious minutes of each working day analysing what one's chief meant, instead of knowing exactly what he meant because he had plainly said so. The Press was getting to the point of finding shades of meaning in the twitch of his lip, since often there was not much else to go on. Press conferences naturally were becoming a thing of the past. Now there was oratory to mam-moth meetings at dramatic places, India Gate, the Red Fort and so on. It saved the bother of answering questions. She found the broad back and turbaned head of Ajaib Singh reliable and comforting as he drove her back to her own Ministry. She took out her handker-chief, blew her nose determinedly, and tried to recall her engage-ments for the afternoon. The future was not after all a yawning abyss. It was, for the time being, a calendar of engagements.

The first thing she saw on her desk was a letter from Ajaib Singh, lying on top of other papers in obedience to her instruction that any matter concerning any of her staff must be brought to her im-mediate attention. 'Respected Sir: Deeply moved always of your noble and kind remembrance of me in matters large and small I am bold to write this epistle. Only to noble high and mighty soul such as your sweet self would I write. Sadly Sir our country is passing through bad days when sons do not so much listen to fathers. I write Sir with bowed head and shame surpassing of my third son who did not obey his mother and me failing many examinations at school. Now he has barely passed Matriculate and what future for him honoured Sir without degree. Therefore only your great name and high office will gain him admission to college and I humbly re-quest this no-good worthless may be admitted to Jammu College near my land and home. Where if he does not succeed in first year I will pull him out and train him in drivery and put him in taxi ser-vice but always preferring him to be educated and above me. May God keep my noble and delightful Sir, your obedient servant Ajaib Singh.' The signature was scratched in spidery Urdu with a very thin nib under Ajaib Singh's letter writer's smudgy black typewriter ribbon. Devi read it all over again for sheer pleasure. No acquaintance of her own social position had ever offered to remove a lazy offspring if he did not make the grade after the first year. Quite a number of them, Devi recalled, might be better suited to 'drivery' than a B.A. degree. However, she knew Ajaib Singh would do exactly as he said, remove his third-born 'no-good worthless' without further ado, and that either the republic of India would have a successful B.A. with a horizon wider than Ajaib Singh's or else a cracking good taxi driver. It pleased her to think that one of her last acts in the Ministry might be a service for Ajaib Singh.

She picked up the private telephone on her desk and dialled Usman's number. He lifted it at the first ring.

'It's me,' said Devi, 'I've just got back from the Cabinet meeting.'

'And how was it received?'

'Only one person talked but the reaction was unfavourable, and I think he was speaking for everyone.'

'You *think* he was?'

'Well, it's all guesswork nowadays. No one owns up to anything.'

'Did the oracle speak?'

'It spoke but I'm none the wiser.'

There was a pause, then Usman burst out laughing.

'My poor Shahbano, you are very out of date, demanding clarity. The world has moved on into a frightful fuzz – of ideas and emotions all clogged up. Catch up with it or – come with me.'

She said, 'I think you'd have been disappointed if your paper had been approved. You're itching to go off with your crazy plan.'

Usman sounded positively jubilant. 'I wish I could see your face, Shahbano. I like it when it has that stern devoted-to-duty look. You get a crease between your eyebrows and a determined set to your jaw. How is it looking now?'

She should feel the warmth and pressure of his hands on hers across this desk, hear the gaiety in his voice the night he had announced his plan.

'I don't have a mirror around. I'm still devoted to duty but I think my duty has changed.'

'Of course it has.'

'You needn't take that so much for granted. It came over me all of a sudden, all by itself, at the Cabinet meeting. I suddenly felt I didn't belong.'

That was the way of big decisions, Usman said. Your rational mind thought them out later, but they were born of themselves, out of some profound realization already there.

'But now I feel I'm in the middle of nowhere and I don't know what to do and it's all your fault,' Devi ended on a childish note.

'What have *I* done?' he was in irrepressibly good humour.

'You with your visions, breaking up the world and making it all over again,' she spilled out and stopped, reminded of Omar Khayyam.

Mind-reading he quoted, 'Ah love, Could thou and I with fate conspire . . .'. Let's meet this evening.'

They met at Michael's, a three-cornered gathering determined to be light-hearted, before the realities of Devi's impending resignation and Usman's uncertain future caught up with them.

'We're making too much noise,' said Devi.

'Make more,' urged Michael, 'it'll keep Mrs. Kartik from looking in to see if I'm lonely.'

Later Michael read them his latest chapter. Usman left him talking to Devi about it and went into the small kitchen. Moti, Michael's young servant, jumped off the stool and stubbed out the gold-tipped Rothman he had taken from Michael's carton. He looked extremely smart in a bush shirt patterned with elephants, hip-hugging pants and his favourite film star's hair style.

'Is everything ready?'

'As you said, sahib.'

Usman pointed to a pile of chopped onion. 'Did I say anything about onion?'

'No, sahib, but if it's meat you're cooking –'

'Take it away.'

'But all meat, the best Mughlai dishes need onion.' Moti was on loan from a restaurant in Karol Bagh.

'I'm improving on the Moghuls,' said Usman, 'and don't present me with garlic either. Where's the fresh ginger?'

He checked the array of spices he had ordered to be ground. Cumin, clove, cardamom, coriander, chili, and finely cut fresh ginger.

'Where's the yoghurt?'

'The yoghurt is for the *meat*?'

'What else?'

'What am I to do with the vegetables? You didn't give any order about those,' said Moti.

'Feed them to the goats. What we need is three kinds of meat and some good roti to eat it with. Unfortunately we've only got time to make two kinds. Where's the mince?'

'In the fridge.'

Usman dumped the cut pieces of mutton into sizzling oil in Mrs. Kartik's heaviest utensil, along with yoghurt, salt and all the spices. He had been taught this recipe by Shivraj's mother. Between religion and cooking he'd learned quite a lot from her. One of the things he'd learned was that while the ideologues talked ideology, personalities like hers and Shivraj's in their different ways took the people with them. Proof that the earth that bore you won everytime. Nothing could get the better of it. The meat was slowly changing colour in the boiling yoghurt.

'I hope the gas isn't going to give out before I finish.' He looked suspiciously at the heavy red cylinder under the kitchen table. If it did there might be a day's wait and several telephone calls to the company agents before the next cylinder arrived.

'We've only had it a week,' said the boy, 'it should last us a month.'

Usman was closely watching the browning meat. Only two things really took your mind off problems, one was a game of tennis because there was no getting away from the ball, the other was cooking, which lulled you into thinking other thoughts. He began thinking of Nadira whom he'd taken out in the car after he had spoken to Devi. His arm was enjoying its release from the sling, and his mood after talking to Devi and realizing his decision was upon him, was calm. Such times, when the unknown with all its nerve-jangling risks stretched ahead, were for mental preparation, the lull the swimmer needed before he took his plunge into the deep. Or as Shivraj's mother had once explained her weekly fasts, as a simple ritual for self-purification.

'Where are we going?' asked Nadira.

'Nowhere in particular. Just for a drive. It's cooler outside at this hour.'

On the way he told her of the decision he had made and his

134

hopes and fears concerning it. There was grass and shade off the road surrounding a ruined tomb of the Tughlak dynasty. He parked his car and they sat down on a stone bench scraped of its white-wash. Telling her was harder than he had expected. He began to see more clearly the difficulties of it for her.

'What do you want me to say?' said Nadira, when he had finished.

She was playing with the handful of daisies she had collected in her lap while he had been talking. Her profile, pure and chiselled, had the beauty of a Moghul miniature. She didn't look at him as she went on.

'With your qualifications and background, we could have had any sort of life we wanted, lived anywhere in the world. The children would have had a good future. We'd have had more money. I don't think it's such a crime to want comfort and security and recognition.' She said it without quarrel or complaint.

'It's true I've had very little regard for those things,' said Usman, 'and of course they matter.'

She would have adorned another man's home, deserved a bro-caded luxurious existence, had money to spend on herself, glittered and shone. Even her poetic talent had wilted with him.

'Well, if you've made up your mind, there's no more to be said about it,' she concluded.

'Darling,' he turned to her in appeal, 'there's so much to be said. We're at the beginning of something that has tremendous impli-cations. I want you with me in this.' His desire for her support and understanding became mixed with his need to touch her tenderly, take her face in his hands, two things he must not mix at this moment.

'What can I possibly give you? You don't need me. You don't need anyone.' The resignation she said it with gave her words a quiet unemotional strength.

'Tell me one thing,' she continued. 'is this a pact between you, with her handing in her resignation and you giving up your job at the same time? Did she persuade you to do this? Is it because of her?'

'Can you conceive of my taking an important step I wasn't con-vinced of myself?'

She looked searchingly into his eyes and was satisfied. 'No,' she admitted, 'But she does have an influence, a terrifying influence, on everything you do. She thinks she owns you. And you behave as if you own her.'

The air, overhung with unspoken accusation so much of the time, cleared slightly as she spoke.

'Everyone has a past,' said Usman, 'and the past has a way of continuing into the present. We can't at some point say it's over and done with. Bits of it linger and they should. It's part of the – perfume of life.'

'I gave up everything when I married you,' said Nadira.

'That you did not. You brought it all with you, your attitudes, your prejudices. We all do.'

Nadira drew a hand across her eyes. 'Very well, Usman. What I mean is her. As long as our life was more or less normal I could put up with her. But now I don't know what to expect. Besides I don't know what you want of me.'

'I want what you never give me, your stubborn uncompromising heart and mind. You know very well what I want.'

She turned to him and said with a smouldering anger, 'And I want yours. But that's given to her. You're quite ruthless about not giving her up.'

Wipe out the past and move ahead. Only those who had no past worth keeping could do that, and only the hopeless had no past. Usman was soon going to involve himself in a massive effort to keep the past, resurrect the best of the past and put it to use. Was he to begin by divorcing himself from his personal past?

'You keep a hold on me too,' said Nadira, 'you know exactly how to handle a woman, what to do with her.'

'A woman?' he repeated 'Would you say I have less – success – with my students, or the men close to me?'

'All right then – people,' she conceded grudgingly, 'you have your successes with people. But that's not what I'm talking of.'

'Believe me, there is nothing for me to give up,' said Usman, 'I am not Devi's lover. I admire her. Has that really ever come between you and me'?

She though of the perfect rightness of his love-making, the precise, almost psychic way he understood the demands of her body, the time and obvious pleasure he gave to it, the impossibility of doing without him. But she would not add to his triumphs by admitting it here.

'There's so much uncertainty ahead,' he went on, 'you and I must depend on each other a great deal. I shall on you.'

Nadira did not reply. They had reached an impasse and he had not been able to give her the cut-and-dried assurance she wanted. He knew he would not try to draw her into this venture with him again. This was final and it hurt. He had underestimated his own vulnerability. On the way home he told her Michael had asked them for dinner and that he had offered to cook it. Nadira had said she would not come. When he left the house, tight-lipped later that evening, he wondered if all comings and goings would now be like this.

Usman became aware there was no sound from the drawing room. He glanced in. Devi was busy with Michael's manuscript, her slippers off, sitting in an armchair with one foot tucked under her. Michael was not there. He went back to his meat. All the yoghurt had evaporated. He poured a cupful of hot water into it, stirring as he did so. There was a peculiar humiliation in not being able to convey your truth, your essential personality to the person who lived under your roof, shared your bed, saw you in all your unguarded nakedness every single day; the person who had more evidence to condemn you than any other had, but who also had glimpses into your striving, your efforts at bravery. Who else saw any of that, and why should the debit side alone figure in the summing up? Yet really the failure was his. Wherever he might have succeeded, with Nadira he had failed. Maybe she had erected an Islamic fortress around her, imprisoned herself, a princess in a tower. But he had failed to reach her, and the failure was his. He put the lid on his utensil and turned the heat low. Moti waited expectantly, his preparations for the mince made. He had, he said, also shelled half a kilo of peas.

'To put in the mince' he said with a grin. The lady, the Minister had said so.

'Oh well, all right,' said Usman defeated, and began to attend to the mince, and was soon engrossed in its transformation from raw red to browning aromatic crumble. Moti collected cutlery and glasses on a tray and went to the dining room to lay the table. The kitchen door was open and after a while Usman heard Michael's voice, followed by Nadira's, cheerfully accepting a drink from him. She came into the kitchen.

'Michael brought me. How is it getting on?'

Usman washed and dried his hands at the sink. He felt a whole-hearted admiration for her will to understand, even if understanding wasn't yet there. It showed in his face, in the keen delight he took in her presence. He took her by the elbows, indicating the glass she held that kept him from coming closer.

'I'm sorry – ' began Nadira.

Usman put a hand over her mouth. 'Don't ever be.' He took her into the drawing room.

14

'Are all the houses you go to as grand as this?' Skinny, wide-eyed
with lively curiosity, prevented herself in the nick of time from falling into the small ornamental pool in the marble foyer. She took
several deep breaths of air-conditioned air, adjusted her slipper
and rushed after Rishad. He walked ahead of her through a hall
lined with pictures, not giving her time to look at any of them.
Pinky's party was in the garden on the other side of the house. A
buffet table covered with a gleaming white satiny cloth extended
down one end of the terrace. White-coated bearers were placing
plates and cutlery on it and three bowls of bought roses with ferns.
Skinny supposed there were no flowers in the garden but she
couldn't see as the flower beds were in darkness. There was a
'shamiana' in the illuminated part of the lawn where drinks were
being served, and next to it in the open a raised platform where a
band was playing and people dancing.

'Isn't Pinky looking super-divine,' said Skinny, dazed.

And loaded with jewellery, noted Rishad. Great clanking chunks
of it. Arvind, smooth, blank and nondescript, would be saying
nothing that mattered for hours on end. Like the rest of them. Rishad wondered how he was going to get through the evening without being rude to anybody. If Pinky hadn't telephoned about ten
times he wouldn't have come at all. Skinny, standing beside him on
the terrace, surveyed the scene. She asked in a small voice, staring
out over the sea of costumes, 'Do I look all right?' Rishad turned to
look at her. She was wearing a sari of some pastel, indeterminate
colour and texture that seemed to become part of her movements.
He had thought of women and their clothes as two separate things.
On Skinny the two had melted, leaving a disturbing image, one
flowing into the other. She wore a fragile silver chain with a medal-
lion on it close to her throat. Rishad had seen hundreds of medal-
lions like it along Janpath, but on Skinny it looked unusual. A

glistening cluster of red glass bangles caught the light every time she moved one slender wrist. She had swept her long unruly hair up into a sleek coil. Flat as paint against her head it brought out the delicate bones of her face. Skinny looked timeless and ageless. He didn't realize he had not answered her question.

'Well, do I?' she asked anxiously.

He gave her shoulder a brotherly pat and said, 'You look fine,' when he meant she looked like platinum in a junk shop. He suggested they get drinks from the shamiana. Confronted with choices Skinny leaned and lingered over them, then asked Rishad, 'What are those people drinking?' He looked across to a group on the edge of the dance floor.

'Different things – gin and something, whisky, as far as I can tell. In this house you can get any known drink, the best smuggled brands. Would you like Scotch?'

Skinny looked genuinely shocked.

He would have explained that Scotch cost the earth and was the status symbol of the upper crust, and that a good few had come this evening just to get drunk on it, only Skinny would have thought it a daft reason for coming to a party. She wouldn't have believed him either. After much brooding, she selected a grey-looking fruit juice which she assured him tasted super. She gave Rishad a little nod and told him not to bother about her, she'd be all right. Rishad, an unfamiliar feeling of responsibility nagging him, was not at all sure about that. The contrast between Skinny and the party, between Skinny and the covetous clawing tinsel world, seemed immense. He left her holding her glass of juice in both hands, looking devouringly around her, yet somehow fastidiously separate from what she saw. Skinny looked down between her feet at the softest, evenest grass she had ever seen, and up there on the terrace was the cunningest floor. She went back to have another look at it with its intriguing pattern of pink and black stone chips all joined together with a sort of crushed sparkle between them that shone in the light.

'Priya!' called Pinky warmly, coming up to the terrace, 'I'm *so* glad Rishad brought you. You *can't* drink juice this evening. I'm getting *married* next week, and this is my last unmarried party. I'll get you a sherry. Don't you want to dance? Come along and meet some people.'

Pinky, so lush and so kind, enveloped in a heavenly fragrance and looking like a vision, took her back into the shamiana, put a glass of sherry into her hand, surrounded her with people, who after the first few words and glances all began talking to each other again and not to her, so that was all right. Skinny raised her first alcoholic drink to her lips with the air of a priestess performing a mysterious rite. The amber liquid softly burned through her, made her feel a goddess. She wanted to stretch her limbs and dance, bestow favours, grant wishes, sing. But she felt shy. Pinky's friends were so smooth and sophisticated. She had had two sherries and dinner was nowhere near being served, but the music sounded louder and louder and the dancers' arms and legs were all over the floor, doing whatever they liked. The girl near her looked as if she were driving a car, and her partner seemed to be drying his back violently with a towel. She went back into the hall to look at the pictures – two generations of Pinky's family, mustached, turbaned gentlemen and vast ladies in enormous frames – and came out onto the terrace again where she stood leaning against a pillar, a spinning lightness in her head from sherry and the pangs of hunger.

The man standing below her caught his breath. She was, he thought, like an Ajanta painting, with those long eyes, that narrow jewel of a face, and her unconscious grace. She had the same young-old quality of mystery and eternity of the 1,500-year-old Buddhist princess in the cave mural. Sushil, who seldom saw anything clearly unaided by alcohol, had had enough to see with startling clarity tonight. He got himself a fresh drink and went up the steps cautiously, glass in hand.

'Well hello,' he said, 'you are a friend of Pinky's I haven't met.'

'That's because I'm not really a friend of hers. Rishad is, the person I came with.'

She was hardly more than a child, and her voice and smile had in no way spoiled the extraordinary effect her looks created.

'And where is this person?'

'Oh somewhere around. He knows everybody.'

'How very odd of him to leave you alone.'

Skinny did not recognize this for the compliment it was.

'He is quite odd in some ways. But I told him not to bother about me.'

'Indeed,' said Sushil, 'you must be the only woman on all the planets to tell a man that. But this odd person you came with did not even ask you to dance?'

'I don't know how. Except like this.'

She couldn't resist showing him. She raised her arms straight above her head, palms touching, then lowered them, elbows bent, to rest on her head in the sensuous immortal gesture of the most ancient school of dance. Sushil's eyes followed it greedily. The posture had narrowed her waist to a handspan, lifted the small crescents of her breasts to curves of alluring promise. He couldn't help noticing the clear-cut classic economy of the movement. The girl was a practised dancer.

The thickset stranger looking so concentratedly at her had a full-lipped fleshy face. Elderly but nice. Skinny did not feel shy and uncomfortable with anyone that old.

'What is your name?' the stranger asked.

'Suvarnapriya.'

'If a thousand poets had dreamed a thousand years they couldn't have dreamed up a more apt name for you.'

'Really?' she was delighted, 'Why?'

'She doesn't know why. This is the most amazing evening of my life.' He offered her a sip from his glass and she kept it, sipping slowly. 'And speaking of antiquity, do you know you resemble the princess in one of the cave paintings at Ajanta?'

'The one who has two left feet by mistake,' she said promptly.

'Yes, only you do not resemble her in that respect. See?' He lifted her sari a few inches. 'Have you ever been to Ajanta? I should like to take you there.'

From her feet to her face she was a collector's item. Between her and the reigning movie queen he had brought to the party and with whom he had sated every gluttonous sexual impulse in the repertoire, Sushil felt he had walked onto another continent of space and air where leaves were in bud and the land lay waiting in a breath-held prelude to a fantastic blossoming. He was seized by nostalgia for the years behind him and a violent irritation with the flesh-trap he was caught in. But with this girl, this scarcely more than a child, there might be a last chance, a breakthrough to another dimension in his career, even a personal future. One of the refreshing things about the child was that she had not even recognized his celebrated face, though it was plastered in technicolour over at least ten billboards in the city and his new film was playing in at least three cinemas.

'How would you like to have a screen test?' he asked, sitting down on the settee behind the pillar, and offering her his glass again. He leaned up against the cushions and invited her to sit beside him. When she had drained what was left in his glass, he put it down on the floor and turned to her to explain.

Skinny forestalled him. 'I'd love to,' she said, 'it would be marvellous. Are you a producer?'

'Yes, and an actor.' He told her his name and comprehension dawned in her eyes. 'You're the girl I want for my new film,' he said.

Skinny gave him her address and said she would have to get her father's permission, and then she leaned back, put a hand on her tummy to stop it growling, and shut her eyes. When she opened them again the fleshy face was very near, breathing onto hers, filling her nostrils with unidentifiable masculine smells. One puffy damp cheek lowered itself against her cool dry one. She turned her face away from it and his lips found hers. They had a pouchy feel like the cushions at her back and they started moving against hers in a rather boring way that was just beginning to be interesting when an exclamation made them move away. Skinny struggled up to see Rishad rigid with anger. He said stiffly, 'Do you want dinner? They're serving it now.' She got up, said goodbye to her companion and followed Rishad to the buffet table. The spread was unbelievable. Kissing was not up to much, she decided, helping herself with pleasure, though one problem had been solved. Noses didn't bump. She took her full plate to a chair and sat down to enjoy her dinner. Rishad, she saw, was fiddling around with a teaspoonful of something, looking like all the furies.

'Goodness,' she said, putting her plate down at last, 'aren't you hungry?'

'No. And if you're ready to go home I'll drop you. If you want to stay on, I'll arrange for someone else to give you a lift.'

'I'm ready.'

It was a quarter to eleven and Bhola Ram, God willing, would not wake up as soon as she came in. For a chap who needed a hearing aid he could hear at all the wrong times.

She said her goodbyes. From a few feet away the actor raised his hand in an admiring salute and a look that made it plain he would get in touch with her again. Outside, and away from the crowd and the band, it was cooler. There was a breeze and a moon they had not noticed in the bright lights of Pinky's garden.

'Do all your friends have dinner so late?' she asked, settling herself comfortably into the front seat of the car beside him, 'I thought I'd die waiting.'

'These are not my friends,' he said shortly.

'Then who is?'

'No one you know. And certainly not this useless bunch.'

'Why do you spend your time with people who don't matter to you?'

'I spend my time with my books. And the rest of the time I can't just disappear from the life I have to lead.'

'Why do you have to lead it? Why can't you lead the life you like? What's to stop you?'

Rishad was driving with his foot on the accelerator. There was no traffic. Delhi was empty, silent, sleeping or dead, but he realized he had to get out of the intersecting roads of Pinky's neighbourhood onto the open road, the airport road, if they were not to come to grief.

'You really are mixed up,' observed Skinny sleepily.

'Not as mixed up as you,' he raged in a low voice, 'wrapped around that disgusting old drunk. Your behaviour was absolutely revolting.

'What was absolutely revolting about it?' demanded Skinny, waking up, 'All he did was kiss me and except he's old and fat and a bit sweaty it wasn't bad. I can't sit around until I'm eighty waiting to be kissed.'

'It was disgusting,' repeated Rishad furiously, his vocabulary failing him.

He swerved violently to avoid a truck speeding toward them, and drove the car off the road. He stopped it with a jerk, throwing Skinny forward in her seat.

'I am going to walk home,' said Skinny recovering herself.

'You are going to do nothing of the kind, and you don't even know where we are.' Thin high noises of dogs whining in a far-off village, and a nearer gruff bark emphasized the loneliness and their distance from human habitation. But she tried furiously to turn the door handle. Rishad wrenched her hand off it. The gesture flung her against him and she was in an iron grip. She did not know whether she heard or imagined him say, 'Don't go' as his arms closed around her. She was hardly able to breathe against him. Rishad's cheek was sweet and hard against hers, his lips firm, and his eyelashes brushed hers when they kissed. She knew she would love Rishad till the day she died. His fingers touched the top of her head and the single clasp that held her hair up came undone. It tumbled, a soft black mass below her waist. Rishad picked up a handful of it, rubbed it between his palms and held it up to his face. 'How beautiful it is. I never knew you were so beautiful,' he whispered.

'I'm not,' she stammered, 'I'm terrible. So skinny. Look.'

She moved away from him and put his hand to her bosom. Rishad unbuttoned her blouse. In the moonlight her breasts looked like pale flowers in bud, sleeping, closed.

'Do you think they'll grow? Sometimes I think they'll never grow.'

'Oh Priya.' He knew with a sharp sweet revelation what strangers foresaw when they looked at her, spoke to her. He knew with the power and thrill of prophecy that she would grow and grow, become a strange and wonderful woman, inside and out. 'Priya.'

It was the first time he had used her name and he said it knowing it meant beloved. They got out of the car and lay down on the hard ground a few feet from it, and Rishad used his small practical knowledge with infinite care as though he had discovered its real use. A long time from now when he became more confident and knew better how to make love to her, their bodies would fit more smoothly and easily together, but nothing ever would take the place, in joy and discovery, of this night. Afterwards they lay peacefully entwined, talking at first in low voices and gradually louder because the dim moonlit plain that fell away from the road was so big and empty and they the only two people on it. On the other side of their car not a single other car flashed past in the night. Priya fell asleep and Rishad lay unmoving, his arms under his head, gazing up at the baffling stars. Only tonight the firmament was peaceful. He felt he had been on a long journey. The future was not all sorted out but at least some of it was clearer. He and Priya had talked, and without ever using the word love they had pledged themselves to something bigger even than their love for each other, something involving the gaunt moonlit plain and the stars above, the impenetrable realm he had tried so hard to penetrate with his mind and reason and never succeeded, the realm Naren understood so well, where people met and communicated and shared each other's pain. He had been mixed up, Priya was right, waiting for that realm to be miraculously revealed to him while he lived his own life in another. Priya had demonstrated the first time he met her that revolution begins with oneself, is not a lesson given to others. Some blindness had prevented him from seeing the obvious and making the only contribution that could matter: a clean break with the life he led, an end to this sterile intellectual participation, and a going over to the other side. He did not know yet where that meant going, but he knew he would never, as long as he lived, go back to the life he lived. He would have to make some plans with Priya first, and he would have to talk to Naren.

15

Pinky looked at the gold watch on her wrist, Arvind's present to her on her twentieth birthday last week. Though Reba and Tazi had left only fifteen minutes ago, it seemed ages. She had not been able to persuade them to stay and it was still an hour to lunch or longer if Rishad and the others did not turn up on time, and no one ever did. Downstairs her sisters had put on the stereo good and loud. Saturdays were so rowdy with them home from school and college and every day was a crashing bore now that she could not go to college herself. College was boring, too. but her friends were there. Saturdays had to be systematically got through. Because Arvind was here for the weekend she could have a lunch party today, thank goodness.

She had gone that morning to the Ashoka to get her arms and legs done, leaving her skin with a polished look, not a hair in sight. When she got back she must have spent half an hour plucking her eyebrows and bleaching the minute hairs around her mouth. After that she had sat, timing it, with her elbows in lemon halves like the magazine said. But all that put together hadn't taken two hours. She would have been bored silly for the rest of the morning if Tazi and Reba had not dropped in. They'd lounged around and smoked, taking care to flush the cigarette butts in the toilet. Pinky had modelled two of her new trouser suits for them and taken out three of her trousseau saris to show them all over again. One, a sexy letterbox red, was a real stunner and they had insisted she put it on. Tazi had said with a sigh that *any*thing would look sexy on Pinky, lucky girl, and they had got into a discussion about sexiness and what it was, agreeing that if anyone had it, it was Madame Kazan, blonde wife of the Turkish Airlines boss, who shopped at the same boutique Pinky did. She had been a model and had a model's figure, no back, no front, but yards of leg, and she tanned herself practically black. Her voice sounded like tyres crunching gravel and she smoked like a chimney. She really was something. When she took a cigarette lazily out of her handbag every male in sight rushed at her with a lighter. A mass stampede, Tazi had sighed. Reba, who had a literary bent, compared her with a eucalyptus, long and blackish-silver, swaying in a literal hurricane of men. Lucky Pinky, Tazi and Reba kept repeating, soon she'd be living her own life, away from prying supervision: no you can't smoke, it doesn't look nice to drink, that blouse is too tight, be home at ten-thirty, of course you can't pose for an ad., are you out of your mind, no I don't mind neither does Daddy but your grandmother would be very distressed or Daddy's third cousin twice removed with one foot in the grave would die of a heart attack if he heard of it, and anyway we don't want our precious little doll-doll to be in an ad. for every 'lafanga' to gape at . . . Soon she would be elevated to wife status and she could do as she pleased. Arvind had a flat in Bombay and his million relations, thank every saint, lived hundreds of miles away in some god-forsaken town of Uttar Pradesh.

Tazi and Reba had asked Pinky to put on the other two saris to show them. They were great heavy brocades costing nearly a thousand rupees each, weighing a ton. She'd probably use each one twice in her life, but they were gorgeous. She'd wear the heavier one at her parents' reception on the evening of the wedding with some of her parent-given jewellery. At Arvind's parents' reception the next day she'd have to wear one of *theirs* and *their* jewellery. Pinky was so *lucky*, with this trunkful of new clothes, and another trunkful she'd been told coming from *them*. Tazi said, 'I bet they'll marry me to some clot who hasn't got two rupees to his name. We don't have Money ourselves.' Reba said the problem was finding a nice man, not money. The worst kind of husband was the jealous kind. She knew, because her aunt was married to one and that go-getter had spent every penny of her aunt's money, and was always accusing her of flirting with other men and thrashing her into the bargain. But everybody apparently didn't react that way, because take Madam Kazan again. *Her* husband was as meek as two mice though she was sleeping around furiously and everyone knew it. Anyway marriage was a change. At least you got out from under your parents. Tazi and Reba were not even engaged.

After Pinky had tried on her saris they had sat around wondering what Tazi and Reba would do in the Dussehra holiday. They wanted to get involved in something but they couldn't think what. And then they had picked up their shoulder bags and rushed off saying they had to go shopping, leaving Pinky alone with more time to kill, half dressed in her petticoat and choli. Pinky looked at her watch again. Only ten minutes since she had looked last. Her saris lay in a heap on her bed for her ayah to fold. She sat down at her dressing table. The room she shared with one of her sisters, air-conditioned and shaded against the afternoon glare, looked edible in candy colours of red, white and pink. Reflected light gave the diamond on her left hand a pink shine and her milk-white pearls a reddish glow, magnetic against the warm honey of her skin. She undid the top button of her blouse and admired the effect of the pearls above the deep cleavage of her delicious bosom. She wondered what Tazi and Reba would do later in the day. Reba might do something interesting. Tazi never did anything but start new diets and fuss over her pimples. Pinky opened her mouth and examined her teeth. Leaning close to her mirror she suddenly saw a single un-bleached hair at the corner of her mouth. With slow deliberation she tweezed it. Now it was nearly time to dress and go down, the others would be arriving. But at two Rishad still hadn't come and they sat down to lunch without him.

Naren's figure lay familiarly still and Rishad stopped in the doorway. If Naren was sleeping, and sleep was so difficult for him, he would not go in, although he had brought fresh sheets from home and this time he wanted to wash and change him. He had brought disinfectant too for his obstinate wounds. He entered the room quietly and went to the foot of the bed. He saw no sign of breathing. There was no envelope of pills in its accustomed place on the suitcase or on the floor near the head of the bed. Rishad hunted around the room and found the envelope blown by a breeze into a corner. It was empty. Naren, his brain told him, was dead. Rishad stood over the bed, his arms and hands cumbrous as huge weights, waiting for a sign of life. He dropped to his knees and took Naren's hand. It felt like a block of wood. His body lay like a statue. His face deeply sunk into the pillow Rishad could hardly see. Was this death? How did one know a man had died, would never open his eyes, move his lips, sigh, speak, laugh, scream under torture ever again? All the taut hidden strings in Rishad pulled discordantly and snapped. He collapsed clumsily to the floor and sat huddled there, holding his hands together to keep them from shaking. Naren had died – from undiagnosed fever, festering wounds, or an overdose of pills. His death was expected. But this was not how Rishad had imagined it would be, another man's death sucking the life and will out of his own body, leaving him desolate. He heard his own voice begin to cry in large wracking sobs that he muffled with his face pressed against Naren's body. At the back of it all a clear stream of reason told him what he already knew, that death was still only death, not more or less than the simple end of living. There was no consolation to be had from it, no after-life, no rebirth, nothing. It was final and forever. If only he had not gone in illness and defeat, with the terrible tapestry of what his torturers had done to him imprinted on his back. Rishad told himself that this, and not the death of Naren, was the worst part, until he was emptied of weeping and realized that the worst part was to be without Naren, the focus and leadership that had meant so much.

After a time, his limbs still alien, his eyes hot and blurred, Rishad tried to recall precise instructions. Naren had told him and the others what to do when he died. They were to take his body to the quarry site in their particular lorry and the quarry workers were to cremate him as one of their own. One more death, unnoticed, unnumbered. But first Rishad would have to find the others and then the lorry driver and wait until night. The longest day he had ever known stretched pitilessly before him. His mind cleared as he began to assemble the details of what he would have to do, and he remembered the other three would be at the Rivoli at Connaught Place today, now. When they had broken up last time the group leader had insisted the tempo must be kept up. Rishad pleading for more time, until Naren was better, was outvoted. He got to his feet, certain he must stop them before the act. Afterwards there would be confusion and a stampede out of the cinema hall and he would never find them.

The road to Connaught Place was a thick jumble of every sort of traffic. A van carrying fifty-foot iron girders jutting dangerously far into the traffic made him jerk his motor-cycle to the right in a terror of collision. Rivers of sweat clamped his shirt to his body, prickled his scalp and rolled down into his eyes. Up further the cyclists held the road. What time was it, why were there so many? He swerved in and out of their tangled columns, got past them only to be trapped into snail's pace behind the creaking heaving trundle of a bullock cart, its driver a round-backed question mark in dirty grey rags. Rounding a bend he came to a crossroad lined with the multistorey offices of several Ministries. The circular garden patch at the crossing, flamboyant with flowers just after winter, lay bare under the September sun, even the grass rubbed off by human bodies. Office workers lay upon it every lunch hour. Then it must be the lunch hour. They lay on their backs, hands over their eyes, dozing, some eating or playing cards. Mercifully the road beyond the crossing was fairly free of obstruction and he drove straining over his machine. He parked his motor-cycle near the Regal cycle stand and bumped his way through a static lunchtime crowd that stood about, solid, chattering, immovable, owning the thoroughfare, blocking it. Past the shops and pavement sellers he turned the corner and not waiting for the lights to change crossed the road dodging the jungle of traffic.

The show had not yet begun. The doors were still open and people milled in the small foyer for tickets. He struggled through. An elbow in his ribs halted him. 'Here you!' said a rough voice. Then he saw the queue at the ticket office, hard to distinguish from the humanity pressing around it, and went back to find his place, his heart thumping heavily with fear and anxiety. 'It's a desperate business,' said a cynical voice in the queue, 'whether it's for food or a cinema ticket or trying to get on a train. You have to be related to a Minister to get anywhere.' Other voices spoke edgily around him, objecting to each other, too many people for good grace, enemies in a cinema queue. Rishad looked in anguish at his watch. It had stopped. There was no clock in the foyer, none that he could see, only huge posters of a red-cheeked, pink-skinned, balloon-breasted heroine, fat calves exposed in a dance. Did the public like them fat because the public was so thin? The queue was shuffling ahead. Where would the others be? They had said they would plant the grenades on the same side of the hall among the last four or five rows. A bell rang and the attendant closed the doors. Rishad found himself at the ticket counter. He pulled out a ten-rupee note, all he had, and asked for a five-rupee ticket. 'No change,' said the man, the window bars cutting his bored face into vertical strips. The bars were new to prevent a grab from the till. They hadn't been here the day they had come to review the possibilities. Rishad racked his memory for the details of the plan. What had they decided? 'All right, keep it,' he told the face. Shoving the note under the grille, he went into the hall.

It had the close stale smell of insufficient airing and packed bodies. All he could see were the two lighted exit signs. He had forgotten which side of the aisle they were going to plant them, which row. There was a car on the screen screaming raucously down an endless road. Abruptly it was replaced by a shiny bead curtain. Rishad looked to the left and right straining to see in the dark. He stood in an agony of indecision. The bead curtain parted. A plump semi-nude cabaret dancer appeared, a singing wail, not hers, issuing from her lips as she thrust her hips into an aggressively suggestive dance. Involuntarily Rishad shuddered, put his hands over his ears and stumbled into the second last row on his left, trying to see faces as he picked his way past knees and feet. It must be the other side then. He got out to annoyed murmurs, apologizing. Back in the aisle he knew it was useless, reckless, to try and stop them. It was too late. He must go outside and wait. Before five more seconds passed he must leave the hall. The seconds passed and he waited, muddled, all sense of time and judgment dropping from him in his agonized determination to stop them. He saw the usher coming up the aisle toward him, heard a deafening explosion, heard screams. He saw the usher curl up and uncurl like a strip of burning paper and tumble grotesquely forward at his feet in the split second that Rishad, his two hands clutching his stomach, fell on top of him.

16

Rishad was born on a morning in late winter, and Ishwar had very nearly delivered his son on his own. The long labour the doctor had predicted for a first born had not taken place. Devi had not panicked, each crest of pain manageable until the end when, taken unawares by the power of this exacting experience, a beseeching cry for help was dragged from her. It was three minutes to eight and Ishwar told her it was a beautiful day. If she raised her head a little she would be able to see the early sunlight, a heavy shimmer on the dew. He helped her to raise herself and she also saw the sweet peas Ishwar had planted three months earlier and that she in her preoccupation with her work and her pregnancy had not even noticed growing. There they were, pre-springtime blooms of sweet serene pastel, each flower's identity merged into a gentle expanse of breathing colour. 'They grew,' she said in wonder to Ishwar, and putting his hand under her cheek she feel asleep.

Michael was beside her bed when she woke. She was on a hard narrow cot in Rishad's hospital room where the ambulance had brought her and Rishad. Michael towered between her cot and Rishad's high bed and the time was some time of night, the room in deep shadow cast by one lamp. Rishad had not regained consciousness. Michael helped her feet into slippers but restrained her from getting to her feet. And his silence and the authority of the arm forcing her to stay seated told her Rishad was dead. The ambulance journey home sealed them off from the night-time road. She next remembered verandah lights, Ajaib Singh helping the attendants to lift Rishad's body and carry it to his room, herself following, then walking into the dining room afterwards with no particular object, only because it led out of Rishad's room. Priya slept at the table, face down on her arms, exhausted with waiting. Devi's hand on her shoulder woke her and the girl raised her head, swollen-eyed, her cheek imprinted with the copper bracelet she wore.

Ram Murti was there, still there, he had not gone home at all, and Kirti stood in the dark doorway, every line of him sagging, his head hung forward as if he had lost control over his neck muscles. Devi turned around and on a chair against the wall sat Mother Carlotta, principal of Rishad's first school, a calm and saintly contact through the years, holding a rosary between her fingers. All mutely assisting at her harsh dry mourning, understanding her famine of feeling where the only agony for the moment was not knowing why Rishad had died as he had. The rest of her felt blank and dark. And then Usman and Nadira came in and Usman took command, setting her free to go to her room and die her own death.

'Why have you given your son a Muslim name?' people had wanted to know.

'He was named by a Muslim friend – a dear good friend.'

'But why?'

There were so many answers. For love and brotherhood and diversity. For Islam which for eight hundred years had been Indian. For expanding frontiers of consciousness. For a country stretching from the Himalayas to the sea. So they had named Rishad Rishad. And he had grown in beauty, unnoticed like the sweet peas, as children do, and had perished as quickly, still in his springtime. Someone was in her room, urging her to get up from her chair. Michael took her by the arm, led her to her bed, made her lie upon it, and what was left of the night travelled slowly toward morning and the cremation of Rishad.

There was no one in the long corridor except Madhu and at the open end of it, a policeman. He turned around and saw her, waved his short stick and called, 'Out, Everybody out' as if there were dozens besides her there. A small giggle escaped Madhu. She blinked and strained to see past the policeman who now stood, legs planted apart, his stick between his hands behind his back, his back to her. She had been reading so long her eyes kept glazing over. There were tatters of maps and posters and bulletin board notices on the floor around her feet, though the bulletin board still hung and flapped in the wind from the doorway and light oblong patches on the wall showed where several photographs had hung. Now they lay trampled and she was stepping on one. Gingerly she lifted her feet off it and began to pick shreds of glass from the soles of her slippers. She had no idea whether it was ten minutes or twenty or longer since the police had arrived in truckloads and poured out and surrounded the college and given the order to vacate. She'd heard it but she hadn't bothered about it. And then there had been a pitched battle with the police when they'd broken up a meeting the students were holding, and all this mess had happened. That she might be the only person left in the building did not alarm her. No warning signals sounded in her any more, not even when she thought of the nightmare room. It wasn't the registrar's room any more. It had no furniture and a tiny grating high up in the wall instead of a window. Outside a band played, hired trumpeters and drummers sweating copiously in circus-bright finery, a procession of flaring gas lights, a man, her unseen betrothed, coming for her.

She bent down to look at the picture she had stepped on. A nice face with faraway eyes and a quizzical smile looked back at her. It was so ruined she could hardly recognize it, but as she picked off pieces of glass and smoothed it out she could see it was Shivraj. It had hung just there, with a quote from one of his speeches in a facsimile of his own handwriting under it. She folded it absently and put it into the pocket of her kurta. The policeman swung round and bawled at her to get out again and she went nimbly past him into the hot, hot day. Somewhere a loud-speaker was blaring. She could hear it as well as its cracked echo further away, 'forces of disruption' 'forces of disruption' 'forces of disruption', a stuck record. There was a loud scratching sound and the recorded voice moved on 'The government has taken over the university. All students will go home' 'will go home, 'will go home.' A scratch and a wheeze and it was repeated all over again. She stopped and listened, then threaded her way casually toward the tea-vendor, the appointed place for her brother to pick her up on ordinary days and where she supposed he would be. A vast bland distance extended between her and the loudspeaker voice, her and the students pouring out of open doors, jumping from ground floor windows, as many policemen as students, a funny patchwork of figures, little knots of them snarling and unsnarling, raising dust, falling under blows, crying and shouting. She found her brother in a furious temper. 'Where have you been? Well, what have you been doing?' he demanded, 'Didn't you hear the call? I thought you had been killed or arrested.' She did not answer immediately, giving him a smile that made him look uneasily away. 'I was reading.' '*Reading!*' Madhu knew he would be thankful when he was relieved of the responsibility of her.

He couldn't ride his bicycle through the crowd. She walked with him beside it, humming to herself. Out on the main road a hot wind lifted thick dust and blew it stingingly across their faces. 'It's like May all over again,' he grumbled, 'Come on, get on. I'm going to take you home and then go to the demonstration.' 'What demonstration?' 'The Vice-Chancellor's' idiot. It's been up on the notice board since the day he resigned. That's why the police came and that's why they've shut up the university.' With his back to her vacant smile he could use his normal conversational tone with her. They could still hear the order 'will go home' 'will go home' carried on the wind like a demented fever bird. He pedalled as fast as he could to dump his bundle and get to the demonstration. He didn't give her a backward glance as he left.

Madhu stood at the door of her home. Here in the alley everything was the same. A mangy dog lay across her path, twitching flies off the pink hairless patches on its flank. Another nosed in a pile of garbage in the gutter, and the garbage can, its lid askew, leaned toward the gutter. A cow, all skeleton poking through skin, lounged across the lane, nudging her as it passed. People came and went, a gaunt pregnant woman, only her stomach substantial with her burden, womb-weary women carrying babies on their hips, dragging others by the hand, old women, used, empty, toothless and bent, their withered breasts swinging loose, no need to cover them any more. Madhu smiled dreamily, full of calm affection for her surroundings. She turned and entered the house where she had been born.

The rough wooden door banged as it closed, the iron chain of its fastener rattling noisily against it, and her mother called out to ask who was there. She replied and went to her room, the corner one off the courtyard. It was all where she had left it, the bundle of rags and sticks collected patiently, the matchbox taken from her brother, the can of kerosene stolen inch by inch from the cooking supply, and added to what she could buy from the bania. She didn't want to run short. Working unhurriedly she smeared her face and arms generously with kerosene and spread it over her clothes as well as she could. She massaged the oil lovingly over her hair and feet and fingers and then she soaked the rags with what was left of it and tied these around her legs and body. She placed the sticks in a big empty tin in the centre of the room. There was plenty of space left by the beds. They were upended against a wall every morning, with the bedding rolled up and stacked on the floor. Madhu sighed deeply and lit the sticks. She had nothing to be afraid of because she knew from reading about witch-burning in the European Middle Ages that often the smoke smothered the witch and choked her unconscious, so that she did not feel her death by fire. She bent, inhaling deeply, exaltation possessing her as she invited the bitter smoke into her lungs and let the fire reach up and catch her clothes and hair.

Three miles away Usman looked up at the sky. It was an intense dark blue, the day dry and burning, the beginning of a succession of death-dealing dry September days in this erratic monsoon, and disastrous for the crop. But Usman was not thinking of the crop. He stood on a small improvised dais with a microphone he hoped would work, at the crossroads near the university campus, and like a cross, with him as its point of intersection, a solid mass of students extended in four directions. They stood in ranks four, six, ten, fifteen deep, he could not tell how many there were. But the gathering was huge and alive and moving continuously at its fringes with new arrivals. Many, he had told Devi, would come with him. It had been a guess. Here was the reality, the hunger and thirst that leapt out at a sign, grasped the shadow of hope with eager expectation, or at least eager curiosity. He was humbled and overcome by the sight. From the day he had had his first dim insight into what he should do as he looked at his destroyed room from behind his desk, possibilities had begun to unfold. Today he saw the live risk of his decision and it made him afraid. He did not fear anything these roused columns might do, only that he might not prove worthy to guide them. He was trembling inwardly, seeking inspiration from the scene around him. He looked behind him and to the left and right. Admittedly a lopsided cross but it was evidence of need and turmoil, a cross he would carry to the end of his life. He had no hard and fast programme to offer these young ones who had responded so passionately to his invitation. He had some suggestions based on a lifetime of study of their problems and a philosophy gained through observation of these and others of their ages. It told him that though they, like their elders, could be indifferent to what went on around them, could walk past the destitute and the dying without a tremor of conscience, and sleep soundly while their neighbour's house caught fire, each would, if inspired, endlessly deprive and punish himself. Individual penance for individual salvation, never mind what happened to the world or your neighbour. It was not his particular way, but it was a way. That was how progress and change might be brought about here, by touching the individual readiness for hardship, the personal desire for sacrifice. Almost accidentally he had released this torrent.

Events had followed swiftly one upon the other. He had announced his resignation and in a tersely worded statement to the press he had given his reasons. He saw the trouble at the university, he said, not as a matter for educational reform only, but an illness of the whole society and one whose remedies would reach out to many areas outside education. He would make common cause with the students and he could not do that from a position of authority. The announcement of the meeting was posted at all the colleges of the university, and something submerged these many months, his reputation, rose up and stood like a sentinel over all his thoughts and actions, giving even his informal remarks a sure touch and sparking off a debate that had already reached other universities. For the first time since Shivraj's death he felt free and master of himself.

He was in his office going through his desk drawers and his steel cupboard, clearing them of his papers. He had dictated letters to his secretary and sent him away to type them. He was leafing through his engagement diary wondering how to deal with the appointments of his official calendar when his nerves told him someone had come silently into the room. A thin, sharp-featured young man stood a few yards from him. He had dirty longish hair, an Adam's apple, tight trousers flaring at the ankles. Usman tensed, his hand closed futilely around the glass paper weight on his desk. He sat rigid and alert.

'I am sorry to disturb you, sir.'

'It's all right.' Usman breathed again. There bad been many such unorthodox arrivals and interruptions since the posting of the announcement, 'come in and shut the door.'

The boy had trouble speaking. He managed to say, 'I apologize for the stone that hit your eye.'

Usman looked at him curiously. 'Are you the one who threw the stone?'

'No, sir. I was not among them. I wish to take their action upon myself.'

Usman, speechless, stared down at the paper-weight to avoid looking at the boy. A sign of grace this, a sign that belonged in the scriptures until one made the scriptures live. When their eyes met he had a glimmering of the adventure of which this was only the beginning, of the profound shared experience that awaited him and these young. He got up and saw the boy to the door, an arm about him.

It was nearly time for him to begin speaking when he saw uniformed men in the distance. One of the students informed him it was the police or perhaps the army – many were steel-helmeted and the boy could not tell. They were massing at all four points of the cross. And Usman knew at once how he, responsible for the lives and conciences he had summoned here, must begin his speech. In a ringing voice that carried clearly over the microphone – silently he blessed its working – he gave a grim warning. Here and now those who were with him must pledge themselves to peaceful action. A roar of voices rose in agreement as he raised both his hands for their response.

The manuscript was back with Michael. Government's comment had been voiced by a Joint Secretary who had a neat turn of phrase. He told Michael it had been his pleasure and privilege to go through it. He had absolutely no criticism of it unless it was the general *emphasis*. Shivraj, you know, was a leader of the *masses*. One couldn't lose sight of that. Of course you were a friend of his, Mr. Calvert, and he was a fascinating man in his individual capacity but how important was that in trying to interpret him so soon after his death? The first accounts would have a big impact on the reading public, would in a sense convey what India stands for. The Joint Secretary, who had taken advantage of a generous scholarship provided by an American university during his student days, and had never before or since spoken to a peasant or a worker, went into a wealth of detail about the relationship of the peasants and workers to Shivraj, and the unforgettable experience of hearing Shivraj address their mammoth gatherings. It was all larger than lifesize, you know, Mr Calvert. And then the political part of the book – well, it didn't go quite far enough, did it? Shivraj had had world-wide contacts with revolutionary movements. His early trip to Moscow had been crucial for his intellectual development. The Joint Secretary did not mention the effect Shivraj's university years in England, or a later trip to China or travels around the world, not to mention his Indian inheritance, had had on Shivraj's intellectual development.

Michael listened, thinking bitter thoughts, while the Joint Secretary spoke in primary colours, words sounding red, hard yellow and flat blue – poster colours – all right on posters but not the medium of any man's character, nor the stuff to convey that one man was many men, and his magic the spark he sowed in the individual imagination, albeit of millions. The book had been 'passed' but Shivraj's successors had found it anaemic, anaemic enough to pass. Not red blue and yellow enough. The Joint Secretary's tone implied that it did not matter as the official biographer would deal suitably, historically, with the subject.

Good luck to him then. Michael shook hands and left the Joint Secretary's office after mutual expressions of good will that barely disguised their mutual dislike and distrust, and chose to walk perversely in the sun some distance before he got into a taxi. He had not been in India very long but in these weeks the book insulation around him had fallen away like scraps of old plaster. Shivraj had walked beside him, sat and shared the converse of his friends, mourned Rishad's death with them. His presence had been strangely real. It had pierced the barrier that protects the writer from the onrush of life and had insinuated life into Michael's careful passion for his work. Shivraj had moved the masses, but the masses were men and women with names and two he knew were still moving, inveterate livers of life caught up in hard new struggles of their own making. Michael wondered what were history-making events and what were not. Shivraj on the public platform swaying the crowd, or the light he had left among his friends? And could the two be separated? Companionship, laughter, the heart's grief shared, the love one had for a woman, were also a chapter in history when, as since Michael's arrival, these were mixed with the anguished concern that India must not lose her taste of freedom. There were eras and characters in history in whom public and private issues met and became one.

The facts about Rishad's death were clearer since Priya had told Devi what she knew, and yesterday the police had come with Devi's sheets, taken from the body of the terrorist they had been searching for. The information was a brutal climax to the disaster, but it had shocked Devi into reaction and relieved some of the intolerable strain of not knowing about Rishad's activities. The police officer waiting respectfully – she was still due deference until she vacated the house and her Ministerial trappings – had been surprised when the fixed tearless look in her strange-coloured eyes sprang to attention. Another woman would have wept. She had made him sit down and questioned him and demanded with a touch of her old imperiousness to be taken to the room where the sheets had been discovered. Michael had gone with her, letting Devi, as she desired, walk up the narrow stair alone, leaving him below among the books. She had come down reconciled to the fact that this was as far as the trail into Rishad's other life would take her.

Devi's house had only an occasional official visitor now, and already looked deserted. It had the stock-stillness buildings and even landscapes get in extreme temperatures. Michael's taxi made an unreasonable amount of noise stopping and re-starting, the only sound in this sleeping neighbourhood during these sun-paralysed hours of afternoon. He found Devi at the dining table making an inventory of government furniture with Ram Murti. The room was in late afternoon gloom, bamboo blinds down, curtains drawn to keep out the heat. The overhead fan was whipping around so savagely that every sheaf of paper had a weight on it to keep it from flying off the table. When Ram Murti collected his papers and went to his office, Devi said, 'I have no idea how well or badly off I am.'

One was apt to think the people one mixed with were as well off as oneself. Michael realized he knew nothing about that side of her life.

'Vijay used to advise me about my small investments. He understands the behaviour of money and knows when it's going up or down before it does. But I stopped asking his advice when he and M. and M. became so intimate. Making these lists with Ram Murti has reminded me I have a dressing table and a few personal items here in the house, and not one stick of anything else or an inch of ground anywhere else. People think I'm rich.'

'Did Shivraj leave much?'

'He left what he had to Rishad. But it was little enough – enough now for a small scholarship fund. I'm thinking of Priya. She mustn't be abandoned.' Devi's sleepless nights had given her face a stiff drawn look. 'It is remarkable how ignorant Shivraj and I were – are – about money. People devote lifetimes to making it, multiplying it, and disposing of it. Money is an occupation all by itself.'

She pushed her chair back from the table and sat with an elbow over the top of it, her hand in her hair. Her gestures remained impulsive and somehow youthful.

'And then I have no skills, Michael. A politician isn't trained for anything else. And an ex-politician is the world's most useless commodity. As our sculptor friend Jaroslav would have said, "It gives me to think".'

'If it's of any use, I'm here,' said Michael.

'Yes, my love, my dearest Michael. But it is peculiar at forty-four to find youself stripped of your fabulous past and your limitless future. Suddenly you're nothing. Even what I have of my present in the way of a reputation – something that people recognize and respect – will be blotted out the day I walk out of this house. That will be the fate of those of us who have minds of our own. Usman will be attacked and reviled and I will be blotted out.'

'You're not so easily finished off,' said Michael, 'I should know.'

The mysterious sexuality of this woman, her baffling attraction for him, was after all no mystery. Anyone who knew her felt it. Her magnetism was simple and primitive. It had a quality of earth, a vein of fire, the elemental indestructible things myths and racial memories were made of. Even her loyalties were primitive. Her un-reasoning attachment for her brother, for example. She was not a woman of ideas. Shivraj and Usman had fed her those. What she possessed was an absorption with living. It would be hers till the day she died, and however long she lived she would die young. And yet this was apparently so unusual a tribute in the modern world that it passed for mystery and magic. Magic was indeed a world men had associated with Shivraj than whom no more human or straightforward being had existed.

Devi said with a sigh, 'That may be true, Michael. But at my age one wants to continue things, not make new beginnings.'

'Genghis Khan began his conquest of the world at fifty, not to mention Usman.'

He came in as Michael spoke his name. He had come straight from his demonstration. He was covered with dust, his face stony, the glitter of an avenging angel in his light eyes as he told them of his anger at the massive police presence and his hideous fear that one wrong move by them would flare into violence and destruction, ending at a single stroke what he had just begun. Fortunately it had not. But step by step he would have to wrestle with the danger that it might, the entire perilous way ahead. When he was more relaxed he described the odd shape the gathering had taken. It had looked like the sign of the cross, a wobbly cross but a distinct one. In his best ironic manner he turned to Michael and asked if even a crooked cross could not be considered a symbol of life everlasting – not that he believed in signs and symbols himself? Michael laughed, 'You'll make a Christian of me yet,' though he knew Usman's words were for Devi, for a pain still too raw to receive open comfort. His careless tone, the whole careless angle of his body, were devices he used to convey what mattered dearly. Devi glanced up, understand-ing him perfectly. She asked him about the gathering and Usman continued talking with a mixture of philosophy and humour about the miracle he believed had come his way, and might in time work its leavening among them – or might not. It was a risk one took, he said, when one gambled for the big things.

Devi had taken the manuscript from the sideboard where Michael had laid it and was turning the pages. The opaque starched white of her sari made her skin transparent by contrast. There was a new delicacy about her, of wounds that would hurt less if she moved and spoke very carefully.

'What did they say about your manuscript?' Usman asked.

Michael told him. But it was no longer important what they had said. The man who had died was Michael's concern alone within the pages of his book, and outside it his own true descendants, those who had understood his life and meaning, would redeem his pledges. An impatience seized him to get back to his work and complete it in uninterrupted solitude somewhere away from the heat. He longed to get to a cottage in the mountains within sound of a stream, to breathe the autumn chill and fragrance. Yet to remove himself from Devi when she needed him would be like tearing flesh.

'You'll want to get on with this and finish it quickly, won't you, Michael?' said Devi, 'You could go to Kashmir. While Ram Murti is still with us I'll ask him to book you and make arrangements. When would you like to leave?'

Her knowing his mind did not surprise him nor that his comings and goings from now on would be their joint concern, and he saw that she would need the next weeks to learn to live with her loss.

Michael went with Usman to the front door and opened it to the hottest moment of the day. No trace of cloud or shadow hovered on earth or sky. An arsenal of heat mounting hourly since sunrise was poised to strike earthward for the kill. In minutes after that the light would subtly change and start losing its fierceness as the day ebbed toward evening and unchained some cool from the stars. The men stood side by side, Usman clasping Michael's hand in his own, and then he strode out, his limp scarcely noticeable, a dusty warrior, to his car. Michael saw his profile, austere as a stone carving, framed in the car window as he drove away. The silence was unnatural and he had the sensation of having stood here in another time, of more than close communion with friends binding him to this scene. He had known it in some deeper sense he could not now recall, and whatever foreignness it once had for him had become too much part of him now to seem so. It contained his biggest as well as his most trivial experiences and much of his conscious growth, and yet ultimately all of this boiled down again to the friends he had made and what they had taught each other. Perhaps the strongest thing in human life was influence, transmittable through one life time or the ages. For a moment Michael saw Shivraj as he had first seen him, on a hillside in Kashmir and then other more personal re- collections of Shivraj flashed through his mind. And Michael thought, perhaps we've been in too much of a hurry to say he is dead.

MORE ABOUT PENGUINS

For further information about books available from Penguins in India write to Penguin Books (India) Ltd, Room 2-4, 1st Floor, PTI Building, Parliament Street, New Delhi-110 001.

In the UK : For a complete list of books available from Penguins in the United Kingdom write to Dept. EP, Penguin Books Ltd, Harmondsworth, Middlesex UB 7 ODA.

In the U.S.A. : For a complete list of books available from Penguins in the United States write to Dept. DG, Penguin Books, 299 Murray Hill Parkway, East Rutherford, New Jersey 07073.

In Canada : For a complete list of books available from Penguins in Canada write to Penguin Books Canada Ltd, 2801 John Street, Markham, Ontario L3R IB4.

In Australia : For a complete list of books available from Penguins in Australia write to the Marketing Department, Penguin Books Australia Ltd, P.O. Box 257, Ringwood, Victoria 3134.

In New Zealand : For a complete list of books available from Penguins in New Zealand write to the Marketing Department, Penguin Books (N.Z.) Ltd, Private Bag, Takapuna, Auckland 9.

NUDE BEFORE GOD
Shiv K. Kumar

Just as Ramkrishna, a painter, is convinced there is far more to life than portraits of fat industrialists and buxom nudes, he is murdered. But his problems don't end there. Under a special dispensation granted by Yama, the Lord of Death, he is able to spy on those he left behind—his unfaithful wife, her murderous lover, his unhappy dog, his jealous collegues.... Just when their actions are beginning to really get to him the plot takes a wholly unexpected twist.

'A most amusing book on a daring subject'—*Graham Greene*